Ray McMickle and the Kentucky Vampire Clan

By

Steve Zinger

ISBN: 1-4140-4462-3 (e-book)
ISBN: 1-4140-4463-1 (Paperback)

This book is printed on acid free paper.

1st Books - rev. 12/31/03

One: Headin' Down

Though it was fashionable to hate Americans, one could certainly find two things to admire about them. One was their rabidly obsessive nature. They had some of the most startling images ever etched into history: Neil Armstrong walking on the moon, Richard Nixon's presidential betrayal, Bill Clinton's presidential betrayal, San Francisco of the Sixties, and who could forget the greatest rock and roll bands ever, the Beatles and the Rolling Stones? (Okay, they're not American, but remember: obsession; if it wasn't theirs to begin with then they made it theirs.)

The single most startling image in American history was, unequivocally and without debate, that grainy, Technicolor image of John F. Kennedy getting a portion of his brain removed by the (alleged)

1

bullet of Lee Harvey Oswald. Such a sweet icon of Americana, the second assassination of the country's leader! But the best part about it was, and this is the second thing one could admire about Americans, was the number of teenagers who became so obsessed with the JFK myth that they had posters up on their bedroom walls and they flocked to semi-factual docudramas by Oliver Stone.

That was the sheer beauty of this entire obsession: it could easily be turned into sheer commercialism.

These were some of the things the Stranger thought about as he sat on the Greyhound heading south across the States. He had nothing much else to do but look out the window and think. It really helped distract him from the smell of the guy sitting next to him. He took another look at him and took his wallet from his bag and put it in his inside jacket pocket.

He'd sat in the bus station most of the night waiting, almost falling asleep, until he could finally get a ticket booked. It was just his luck. He was trying to escape and this was the one night of the week that no busses were running between 2 am and 6 am.

And, to his complete disappointment, he was still utterly fucking bored. But he certainly wasn't going to turn back. Obsession, you might recall.

He made his decision only a couple of nights ago. He picked up and left his shit job at the video store, and you know it really wasn't that difficult saying good-bye to eight dollars an hour? He was ready to fucking end it all, and was at his ropes end with life. And it wasn't any frustration, or lack of motivation or even legal or money problems. It was life's emptiness. His best friend had moved away and he had lost touch with most of the others for various reasons both uninteresting and petty. He looked around and said 'Fuck it.' He had to get out of here. But there really wasn't anything special about that. Certainly over ninety percent of Canadians wanted to get out of Winnipeg. Boring little frozen shit hole. Winnipeg was the asshole of Canada.

So he grabbed the first bus out and he didn't have any idea where it was going.

"Just head me south," he told the lady at the bus depot.

"Sixty-two fifty," she said, and he handed her his Visa. The Stranger figured he had maybe two months to rack it up before they cut him off. He got on the bus and sat down, not even paying attention to the other passengers. And, just to ensure his obedience to his new direction in life, he didn't look at the ticket until the bus was well on its way.

The bus ended up curving eastward to Chicago, and that's when he began to wonder where it was he actually wanted to go. He got up (his first mistake, because that's when he noticed the smelly guy next to him, and his stench never left his nose since) and went to the driver, an incredibly obese man, and asked him where he was headed.

"Guessin' you got an open-ended ticket, huh?" he said.

"Yeah," said the Stranger, his voice sounding dead.

"Lemme have a look see." He handed the driver the ticket. "All the way south. Well...this bus is heading down to Florida, if south is where you wanna go."

"Florida...huh," he said, nonplussed.

"Not your cup a tea? Well, were hitting Chicago soon, if you wanna decide by then I could tell you what you oughta do. No idea where you wanna head?"

"Not a clue."

The driver gave a laugh and slapped the wheel, saying he wished he were young again.

"Best thing to do son, is just pick a city and head there. Otherwise you might end up where you don't want to be."

"Point taken," he said and sat back down. About an hour or so later, just dying from the stench of the filthy man next to him, he got back up and went to the driver.

"Decide where you want to go?" he said.

"No, the guy sitting next to me just stinks like someone took a shit on an onion."

"That's what happens when you go all spur of the moment. Life's got all sorts of surprises, ha ha!"

He took a deep breath, because, well, he finally could, and looked out upon the endless stretch of highway before him.

"Did you have a question, son, otherwise you got to sit back down."

"No other seats on the bus, huh," he said, looking behind him with only the littlest flicker of hope.

"Not a one, son. You're stuck where you are."

"How long till Chicago?"

"Another two, maybe three, hours."

"Fuck." He took a deep breath and went back to his seat. It was the longest three hours of his life.

The bus arrived in Chicago and he nearly fell out of it, his lungs praying for oxygen. He spotted the driver shoveling handfuls of Ho Ho's into his mouth and went over to talk to him.

"I think I know where I want to go," he said.

"Atta boy," he said, cake spitting from between his lips. "Get some direction."

The driver beckoned him over to the bus and, wiping his chocolatey hands on his pants he pulled out a route map and they leaned over it.

"Meridian, Mississippi."

"Well," he said, his tongue and lips smacking with chocolate and filling, I can take you most of the way down, then you'll have to transfer. I can have your ticket stamped at the booth for you."

"No chance of me getting on another bus, eh?"

"Kid, I'm doing you a favor by letting you transfer. Your seat's supposed to be with me until the end of the line. You's best hold your nose the rest of the way!"

"Fucking hell," said the Stranger, but things couldn't get much worse, could they?

The Stranger sat down next to the fart bag and after a moment sensed he was looking at him. Why in God's name did he smell more when he was looking at him?! He slowly turned his head, knowing he would instantly regret it. The man's mouth broke into a grin, his lips black and cracked and his teeth outlined brown.

"You're going to be my riding partner," he said. Chicago, Chicago...the Stranger looked out the window and prayed for a producer from Jerry Springer to come lead this man to deliverance. He cursed the flea market that sold him that gray tank top.

"I was kind of hoping to just look out the window, rather than talk," said the Stranger, trying to be polite while conserving his breath.

The pungent passenger looked a bit dejected and he lowered his head, his greasy black and gray hair hanging from his head like a dirty mop. He lifted his bag and seemed to glance into it, then said, "Can you fix my pet iguana?"

"Oh for fuck's sake!" cried the Stranger, nearly jumping over him to get out of the seat. Every head turned because of his outburst and he caught a glimpse of the driver looking in his rear view mirror at him. "The guy's got a dead iguana in his bag!"

"Son, don't make me come back there," said the driver. The Stranger walked up to him and tried to make him see the blindingly clear voice of reason. "Son, you're stuck here till I get you to about Alabama or them parts, then you can transfer and head over to Baton Rouge."

"He has a dead carcass in his bag and it fucking reeks," he argued.

"I'm sure the rest of him smells just as bad. What he's got in his bag is his business. This is America."

"How much longer till Alabama?"

"Hm. About nineteen, twenty hours."

He said, "Holy fuck," then sat back down. He tried to ignore the guy's ramblings, looking out the window, trying to picture all those grainy images of American history, trying to remember that he was obsessively trying to get to somewhere new, different.

Then he figured the best way to pass the time was to sleep, and he did, and his dreams were of flies on a garbage pile. He finally woke to a jolt and it felt as though the grease bag next to him also gave him a bump. He opened his eyes to the grinning, blackened face and rotting teeth.

The bus had stopped. The driver got up and said, "I have to go for a 'pee' break," grinning like a child who was proud he could go on his own, then stepped off the bus. It was day, so the Stranger figured he had slept for only a couple hours or so. Some of the passengers had followed the driver off the bus to stretch their legs, and the Stranger did the same. He squeezed by the stink bucket and rushed out for some air.

"You coming back, right?" he called. "You gotta be my riding partner!"

He got punched in the face as soon as he was off the bus because the heat was so unbearable and sticky, and the dust from the side of the road made it that much worse. He took a look to the distance and found it hard to believe that there were mountains and lush trees within view.

"It is damn hot here," he said to the bus driver. He stood abreast of him, facing the opposite direction.

"Son, I'm taking a piss here and it's turning to steam. You don't have to tell me it's hot." The bus driver jiggled and zipped up. "You might wanna sit back down, we'll be going soon."

"Where are we, anyway?"

"Kentucky."

"Getting there," said the Stranger, trying not to sound too desolate. And why should he be anyway, now that he was free of the constraints of the cruel real world? He went back to the bus and sat down beside Stink Face, who was quiet for a minute as he stared at him then said, "I got something to show you mister." He tugged on his sleeve.

"Buddy, I don't care about your dead iguana."

"You wanna see something soft mister? I'll show you something soft."

The Stranger turned, ready to smack him one, but he grabbed his hand and pointed to the front of the aisle.

"I just thought you might wanna see a pretty girl, mister."

"Hel-*lo*, beautiful," he whispered to himself, not even caring about the filthy hand that gripped his wrist. If he hadn't been so overwhelmed with awe he would have kicked himself for not seeing her come onto the bus. She had long, dark red hair and with each step her hips moved and he felt his head sway and his heart beat. "I have got to get a closer look at that," he said and grabbed his carry-on bag, slung it over his shoulder by the strap and then went to chase the skirt.

The stink face said, "Hey mister! If you don't come back, write me letter you hear? Just send it to Jesus!" He sat back down in the seat and chewed a piece of iguana from his bag.

The woman with the dark and wavy red hair rounded a corner and the Stranger broke into a jog so he wouldn't lose her. When he finally rounded the corner she was a lot father away than he would have expected her to be.

You could tell the town was a small one, though it wasn't really run down or anything. But the streets were fairly sparsely populated, one general store and all that.

She turned and went into one of the shops and he ran to the door and went in behind her. But she wasn't there. He tried the next shop and then the previous one but after about five or so tries he gave up. He'd lost her.

"Fuck. Fuck, fuck, fuck." He threw up his hands in frustration then slapped them back down at his sides. He adjusted the shoulder strap of his bag then started to walk back to the bus. It was incredibly hot and he saw an old-fashioned Coke machine but didn't have any change and didn't have time to stop and make some. He rounded the corner and-

"Son of a bitch!" he shouted, and banged his fist against the brick wall of the building. "You fat, Ho-Ho eating piece of shit!" He threw his bag down in contempt and frustration. The Stranger wiped his face and took a deep breath, then picked up his bag again and sat on the curb up against the wall. The bus, of course, had left without him.

"Well," he said to himself. He checked his wallet to see how much cash he had. Hundred bucks. Canadian money, mostly. Enough for a few drinks and a room, if they would accept his cash.

He got up and slung his bag over his shoulder, then put on a pair of black sunglasses because the sun was so bright. He went back around the corner and-

"Jesus!"

"Wow, mister, you remembered my name. I knew you wouldn't get back on the bus. So I didn't want to leave my ridin' partner."

"Don't sneak up on me like that," said the Stranger.

"Did you find the pretty girl, mister?"

"No," said the Stranger, tersely. He started to walk and Smelly Jesus followed. "Look, I really don't want any company."

"I could be a good help to you, mister," said Smelly Jesus. "I know a lot of tricks on gettin' by."

"Hey, no offense. But I just want to be alone. I came here to get away."

"But I'm your ridin' partner now, mister," said Smelly Jesus, his tone of voice becoming a little forlorn. "You can't never ditch on your ridin' partner..."

The Stranger stopped walking and put his hand to his forehead, feeling a little guilty. Why did he have to have a heart? Having a heart always got people into trouble.

"All right," he said, trying to work out some compromise that didn't involve him keeping company with Smelly Jesus. "You wait on this street corner here. I'm gonna go look around a bit, find out where we are."

"Oh, that's easy, mister! I saw the sign on the way in. We're in Lebanon Junction, Kentucky. Bullet County. I know this place cause this town's farther from any town than any other town is. You're in the right place if you wanna get lost."

"Right, well. If it's all the same I'm gonna look around anyway."

The Stranger adjusted his shoulder bag again and started to walk away, looking around. Smelly Jesus hopped along beside him, and he pulled out a harmonica and began to play.

"You go head and look around, mister. I'll wait here for you.

I'm your ridin' partner so I ain't gonna ditch on you!"

Then he blew on his harmonica and began to sing:

When that mister walks away,

All the monsters come to play!

Lebanon Junction feels so far away,

Hope he sees the light o' day!

"Well," thought the Stranger. Solved that problem. Smelly

Jesus' harmonica playing faded into the distance and the Stranger

looked back to make sure he wasn't being followed. Smelly Jesus had

claimed the street corner and kept crossing back and forth playing the

harmonica, singing his senseless tunes.

Two: The Place Forgotten by God

The Stranger fingered the money in his pocket and thought about the cottony feeling in his throat. He walked down the main street of the town looking for a bar so he could by a drink. A police car slowed as it drove past him in the opposite direction, the cop looking at him as he looked back.

There certainly isn't much in this town, thought the Stranger. Almost dead. He finally found the bar he was looking for and went in.

The bar was so dark and dusty it was like going from day to night. The wooden floors almost looked blue in the dark. The door slammed shut behind the Stranger and caught the attention of the few people in the bar that were slumped over their drinks. The Rastaman bartender smiled at him from under tree shaped dread locks and continued wiping the counter.

"'Ey, mon," he said. "Why don't you come sit down before da door smack you in da ass?"

The Stranger walked in slowly, then sat down at the end of the bar. Two men eyed him from the other end, their eyes glassy with drink.

"What'll I be gettin you, mon?"

"Beer. Really cold."

"That's de only kind," said the Rastaman. "My name be Scooter. They call me Scooter because I deliver da goods. You need somethin' transported, I get if from dere to here for you."

"Thanks, Scooter."

"Tree dollars for da beer, mon." The Stranger put three plus a tip on the counter. "You have a name dere strainja?"

"Yeah. Yeah I do. Everybody has a name."

"And what be yours?" The Stranger felt as though the two men at the end of the bar were leaning in closer to listen.

"Roy," he said quietly. "Nothing special. Just Roy." He took a pull from his beer to ease his parched throat. He noticed the men looking at him from the other end of the bar and he tipped his glass in a toast and took another drink. They neither moved nor acknowledged him. "Who're those guys?" he asked.

"Them guy's is Reg and Donny-boy," said Scooter, loud enough for them to hear, which made the Stranger cringe. He chugged down a few more gulps of beer to relax himself.

"So," he said. "I'm guessing you're not from here Scooter."

"No, mon. And you neither. What you doing here?"

"Just passing through. Heading to Meridian, Mississippi."

"Yes, mon, I was just passin' through here and that was tree years ago. Nobody passes true Lebanon Junction, Kentucky, mon. How you be passin' true?"

"I missed my bus," said the Stranger. Scooter leaned his head back and laughed a sinister Rasta laugh. "Hahahahahahahaha!"

"Dere be no busses passin' true Lebanon Junction, Kentucky, Mister Roy boy stranger man!" Scooter wiped the counter with glee.

"You be here 'cause da fates say you here. And you learn life biggest lesson: never leave da bus when da driver goes to take a piss!"

"So there's no bus that passes through here," stated the Stranger.

"Not a one, mon. De only greyhound we see is da one you cook up for da dinner table."

Scooter wiped away at the counter top and the Stranger slumped back in his chair, dejected.

"Meridian, Mississippi," he said. "What the fuck does Meridian mean?"

"It means somethin' that stand still an' spins," boomed the voice of Reg from the other end of the bar.

"Meridian," said the Stranger.

"Yeah, 'cause when you smash someone's skull in, you're gonna be left spinnin' in circles."

Reg got up and put his hands on his hips. Roy was amazed he found them so fast under his Kentucky fried fat, his gut hanging over his jeans. Needless to say, he wore one of those baseball caps with the mesh backing.

"Reg, mon, you sit your ass back down on da seat. Leave da Stranger alone."

"Scooter you nigger bastard, shut the fuck up or I'll split your head open."

"Reg, mon. Get out of me bar until you sober your brain up and clean up your mouth. Good Lord knows you don't need no language like that."

Reg just stood there, unwavering, his eyes full of violence.

"I call de deputy, Reg. I mean it. He take a bite outta you."

Reg backed down after another moment and gestured for Donny-boy to follow him out. He passed close to the Stranger and, before Roy could do anything, he knocked over his chair. Roy hit the ground with a thud. His ass throbbed and a burst of light blinded his eyes as the two men left laughing.

Scooter was around the bar to help him up.

"You all right, mon?"

"Yeah. Fine."

Scooter took him by the arm and hauled him up. The Stranger dusted himself off.

"No chance in you driving me out of here, Scooter?" asked the Stranger.

Scooter tightened his grip on Roy's arm, said, "Listen, Roy boy, you get your things and get out, cause nobody passes true Lebanon Junction. Dis place a hot hellhole, you hear me? Get out now-"

The light flashed in again and the two men looked towards the door. A bold, black figure was outlined with the sun at his back, and he tipped his hat as though saying hello. The door slammed closed to block out the light and Roy saw the uniform with a gold deputy's star on the left chest.

"How ya'll doing," he said. Neither man answered. The Stranger just dusted himself off. "Scorcher of a day out today." He looked as though he were chewing something.

Perhaps cud, thought Roy.

"You must be the Stranger I saw walking earlier," said the deputy. "I'm Deputy Kuthrow." The deputy didn't extend his hand in greeting, just adjusted his gun belt. "Ah trust you'll be moving on soon, son. Once you're done your beer."

Roy picked up his bag and slung it on the back of the chair.

"You runnin' me out of town, deputy?" he said, grabbing his belt while trying on his best John Wayne imitation.

"Ah'm just lookin' out for my town, son. You've been here less than two hours and you're causing trouble. And besides, there's no place for you to stay here."

"I know, I know. Nobody passes through Lebanon Junction."

"Where you headed, son?"

"Meridian, Mississippi."

"You best be getting on. Next town's miles away and the sun sets in a few hours." The deputy held the door open for the Stranger. Roy put on his sunglasses to relieve the blindness, then picked up his bag and slung it back over his shoulder.

"Guess I am getting run out of town. Nice meeting you, Scooter. Thanks for the drink." Scooter nodded from under his tree-shaped dread locks. Roy walked towards the door, trying to ignore the fact that the deputy was eyeing him the whole way, but he stopped for a sec just before he went through the door. It was the heat that had stopped him, the choking Kentuckian heat that was as hot as the sun was blinding.

"'Ey, mon! You get out of here and forget you ever heard the name Lebanon Junction! Dis is a place forgotten by God, Roy boy, you run and-"

"Scooter," said the deputy, calmly cutting him off. "Shut up or I'll arrest you for being a nigger."

The Stranger jumped out of the doorway because the deputy had slammed it shut. He went to try and open it, but it had been locked, and he was stuck in the unmerciful heat.

Roy began to walk down the road, not really sure anymore which way was out, or which way he should go. This was certainly a strange and unfriendly little town. Thankfully there seemed to be no sight of Reg or Donny-boy, so he was safe.

After a few minutes walk, Roy decided to go into one of the shops to see if the clerk could help point him in the right direction. He opened the door to a shop called Karl's and there was a little bell that jingled to announce his entrance. The clerk behind the desk looked up from reading his newspaper.

"You must be Karl," said Roy.

"That I am," said Karl.

"Wow. You've got a fucking arsenal in here."

"This is a gun shop," stated Karl. He went back to perusing his paper. "Can I interest you in an AK-47?"

"Actually, I'm just here to ask for directions," said Roy, marveling at the collection beneath the glass-topped counter. "Which way is south?"

Karl pointed brusquely.

"Ah. Thanks."

"Ah'd hurry up and get out of here before dark, stranger."

Roy left the store, the door jingling closed behind him. He shuddered.

"That southern accent is really starting to creep me out," he said to himself, and wiped the sweat from his brow. He started back on his original path, which was also the way Karl had pointed.

Three: The Great Grey House

Roy came to the end of the road, and there was a sign that said:

BULLITT COUNTY

LEBANON JUNCTION

MILE 0

Then just off to the right, another that read:

(Blank)

75 miles

Someone had thoroughly scratched out the name of the town but no matter what it was, seventy-five miles was plenty far. He followed the arrow and turned right, trudging on through the heat. His mind had obviously been affected, otherwise he'd have questioned the fact that

there was no indication of a town in the other direction despite the fact
that there was a road that way.

Eventually Roy had the feeling he was being watched, quite
opposite from the feeling of being outcast and ignored in this
godforsaken place called Lebanon Junction. He looked up and saw a
woman sitting on the porch of a great grey house. And he stopped. Her
hair was...long, wavy, red. A hand fan hid most of her face.

"Hey there, stranger," she called to him. Roy turned and went
up the walk, trying not to be too eager. Ironically, on his way out, he
had finally found the girl he'd chased in here. He stood over her and
she slowly pulled the hand fan away from her face.

"I, oh..." stuttered Roy.

"Well, don't look so disappointed honey, ah ain't that ugly."

"Oh, no, it's not that, it's just that I thought you were someone
else."

"Someone much younger, I bet, hm?" Roy searched for
something to say, delaying by scratching his head and adjusting his
shoulder bag. "That's okay, honey, ah know my own age. It just means
ah'm more experienced with men. So where you headed, stranger?"

"On my way out of here. Headed to Meridian, Mississippi."

"Well, that's an awful long walk, mister! Why you in such a hurry to leave, anyway?"

"Well," said Roy, sticking out his chest, "deputy wanted to run me out of town. I was causing trouble soon as I got in here."

Hollywood, here I come! thought Roy. The door to the big grey house creaked and they both turned.

Before Roy could get a glimpse of who it was the red-headed woman snapped, "Close that darn door, Milly!" The door slammed shut.

"Well, stranger, I haven't been as hospitable as the south is known for. My name is Mesmerelda." She extended her hand.

"I'm Roy," said Roy, and he took her hand.

"You're supposed to kiss my hand slowly and gently. It's the gentlemanly way."

"Oh. Okay." Roy leaned down and kissed the back of the woman's hand, feeling the soft and soggy old flesh.

"Now that Deputy Kuthrow is just a nitty old bitty," said Mesmerelda in her high-pitched tones. "He's just a stickler on account of we hadn't had a murder in this town for near on fifty years now. He obviously wants to keep it that way. So he's kind of harsh on travelers. But don't worry, ah got some pull with the deputy. Why do you wanna go to Meridian anyway?"

"I don't know. Just somewhere to go."

"You do know it means a spinnin' axis," she stated.

"I've been informed," said Roy.

"Well, stranger. Or pardon me, Roy. You're certainly welcome to stay here tonight. Ah run a lodgings house for people like yourself. Ah could have one of my girls take care of you."

Roy swayed his head from side to side for a moment, made some funny little gestures with his lower lip, then said, "Thanks anyway, Mesmerelda. I don't think this is my kind of place. I better just get out of here. And he began to walk away."

When he got to the sidewalk, Roy took a glance back at the red headed woman named Mesmerelda. She fluttered her hand at him in a wave.

"You come back if you change your mind!" she called. Roy smiled at her. Then stopped. The door had creaked open again and he

28

tried to catch a glimpse of the girl named Milly. Was this the other red

headed girl? The one who'd lured him off the bus and got him into this

mess anyway? But Mesmerelda noticed him noticing and as soon as

she glanced back the door snapped shut again. Roy continued on his

way.

Four: South's That Way Boy

He walked along the dusty side of the road, paying no mind to the road itself. The houses began to thin and he figured he was finally out of this strange, godforsaken town. Now if only he could escape this heat! But Roy had his head tilting back and, his eyes looking at the clouds and his thoughts in them, he didn't notice the road ahead of him and stepped in a pile of shit.

"Fucking shit," he said appropriately. "Damn it." He scraped off his shoe, sliding it across the dusty roadside and got a pile of leaves to put to the unenviable task. After wincing his nose and muttering profanity for a few more minutes, he tossed the shitty leaves aside in disgust. He continued his walk, and he noticed he was behind a line of shops and decided to see if he could get a wet nap or something-*anything*-to make his shoe somewhat presentable.

"I knew you'd come back, mister," said Smelly Jesus.

"Oh shit," said Roy, no longer willing to mask his distaste of the foul, fetid man. He threw up his arms and tried to turn as though he could sneak away before he was seen, obviously quite impossible.

"What's the matter, mister, you don't wanna be my ridin' partner no more?"

Roy put his hand to his forehead, frustrated, and took a few steps away. Smelly Jesus smelled, and he couldn't escape that because now <u>he</u> smelled. He'd followed an apparently straight road out of town for nearly an hour and came full circle to where he'd begun. Smelly Jesus played the harmonica in his ear and that didn't help one bit.

"Mister, you gonna regret not being my ridin' partner. I know way hell how to survive on the streets better than you."

"Look, I'm just trying to find a way to get out of this town."

"You damn well better, mister. See, I can see things. Things other people can't. This place's got a hold on you. You better leave this place quick, mister. Real quick."

"Oh yeah? Or what?"

Smelly Jesus blew on his harmonica and laughed maniacally. Then the deputy's car pulled up.

"Boy, ah thought ah told you to get on out by now," said deputy Kuthrow, slamming his car door shut.

"I was deputy, I just got turned around, I'm leaving."

"Well, south's that way boy," said the deputy, thumbing over his shoulder.

"I know, I just came from there."

"Then you're heading the wrong way, boy. Best get a move on. And take your smelly friend with you."

They stared at each other a moment.

"Ah wanna see you walk, boy."

"He isn't my friend," said Roy, slinking off under the watchful gaze of the deputy.

"That's it, mister! You ain't my ridin' partner no more! You're gonna regret it, mister!"

Smelly Jesus played his harmonica and taunted the Stranger with a song:

Stranger walked 'way cause I smelled like shit,

Come next day he'll sure regret it.

Gonna keep walkin' round in a loop,

Come nightfall his smile will droop!

"Ha ha!" called out Smelly Jesus. "You're gonna be sorry, mister! I got a red onion with your name on it!"

"Fucking nut case," Roy muttered to himself. "Smells like shit and onions."

Roy kept walking because, well, he had nothing better to do. The deputy was eyeing him, making sure he was heading south, whichever way that was, and he was certainly eager to get out.

Meridian, Mississippi, he said to himself. It sure had a nice ring to it, much better than Winnipeg, Manitoba. It was somewhere to go anyway.

He walked along and noticed how dead the town was. Well, tried not to notice, but it was better than noticing the smell of his shoe or the lingering stench of Smelly Jesus. And why the fuck hadn't the deputy run him out of town either??

It wasn't really that small a town either, just that it was pretty empty of people. No people, actually, Roy noticed. Except for the few he ran into. He had a strange, prickly sensation run up and down his spine. He really had to get out of this town. Lebanon Junction, Kentucky. He'd never heard of it. It was really creeping him out. So he walked faster.

"Psst."

"What the-?" He stopped.

"Psst!"

Roy didn't recognize the place at first, nor could he find the source of the 'psst.'

"Psst! Roy boy! Over here, mon!"

"Scooter!" said Roy. "How the hell-?"

Scooter put his fingers to his lips and shushed him.

"Keep it down, mon, dey should not see me talkin' to you."

"I thought the deputy beat the crap out of you or something."

"Nah, mon. You been watchin' too much Cops on Fox. I see you walkin' and I say to you, mon, get out of da town."

"I'm fucking beat, Scooter, I been walking half the day. I figured I might take up an offer of the lady at the end of the road and crash the night."

"No, mon, don't even fockin' tink dat. You get da hell out of dis stinkin' hellhole. Nobody here by no accident, da fates brought you here and da longer you stay the more hold they have upon you. You just get out and walk and you get away before sundown. Go, Roy boy, move your filthy ass!"

"Scooter, what the hell are you talking about? Let me come in for a drink or something."

"No, just get away now, Roy boy, and stay da hell away from dat house!"

He slammed the door in Roy's face and before Roy could try the handle he heard it click locked. He banged on the door and yelled, "Scooter, open up!" But it was as though no one had ever even been inside.

Roy was at a bit of a loss. He decided to just say to himself, "This is fucked," and shake his head and continue walking.

Five: Oh, silly, there ain't nobody there!

It wasn't long before he came to the end of the road again, and he noticed the grey whore house staring at him from over the trees and fences.

"Let's try this again," he said, and took the right turn instead of the left. But before he'd even got within view of the grey house a bouncing blond girl with pigtails intercepted his path.

"Hey there, stranger!" she said, her voice full of exuberance.

"Howdy," said Roy, trying to fit in with the local yokels.

"You're Roy, ain'tcha?"

"Um, yeah..."

"Hi! Ah'm Millicent. Millicent Gifford. Call me Milly, though. Mesmerelda saw ya'll coming up the road and sent me to get you."

36

"Well, I-"

"You must be tired and all from walkin', and the evening's settin' in soon. Why don't ya'll come on in for a drink and rest up the night?"

"Oh, um, sure, I guess," said Roy, looking around for the group referred to as ya'll. Scooter's warning seemed to have floated upon deaf ears. That and the fact that the blond girl Milly had hung her finger from her lips as she twisted her hips to and fro. "Yeah. Yeah I am tired. I'll come for a...drink..."

"Well, come on! What ya'll waiting for?" Milly grabbed his hand and began to pull him along.

"I-hey did you see someone there?" said Roy, looking over his shoulder.

"Where?" asked Milly. "Oh, silly, there ain't nobody there!"

"It's just that I haven't seen many people in this place at all," said Roy.

"You're just being a silly nilly," said Milly. "There's nobody there. I think this Kentucky heat's getting to you."

"Woah, stop. Just stop. Milly, where are all the people in this town?" said Roy, pulling his hand away from hers.

Milly put her hands on her hips in utterly southern frustration and said, "Stop being so neurotic! Everyone's inside on account of this heat. Geez!"

She took his hand again and walked him to the great grey house.

"Besides, a few days from now, these streets are gonna be packed with people!" said Milly, in her usual excited way. Roy stopped walking again.

"What do you mean?"

"For the Woolly Worm Festival! People come round here miles every year for the festival. If there's one reason Lebanon Junction, Kentucky exists it's for that festival."

"So you mean to tell me that the deputy's trying to run me out of town tonight, just so a bunch of hicks can pile into town for some hokey party?" said Roy, completely aghast.

"Deputy's just an old-fashioned kind of guy. He hates loners and such, so he probably pegged you as a troublemaker from the get go. Now are you gonna get in for a drink or not?"

She grabbed his hand once more, her grip iron and almost painful this time, and nearly dragged him up the steps of the porch to the grey house. She creaked open the door and peeked in like a teenager sneaking around with a forbidden boyfriend.

"Okay, c'mon in," she said, her voice uncharacteristically quiet. Roy stood in the front lobby, looking up and around. Typically southern gothic style of house, but it was incredibly beautiful and intoxicating nonetheless.

"Wow," said Roy. "Oak floors, wine-coloured velvet curtains, crystal light fixtures."

"Ah know, impressive, ain't it," said Millicent.

"Very," said Roy, running his hand along one of the curtains.

"Now ya'll just wait here and ah'll get you something to drink, y'hear???"

"I hear."

Milly scampered off and Roy watched her ass nearly falling out of her short short short short jean cut-offs. He waited and took a few distracted steps around, waving his hands at his sides to occupy himself as he looked around at the impressive decor.

"So, you finally decided to stay after all."

Roy turned around, a bit shocked by the voice from above. He looked up to see Mesmerelda standing at the top of the semi-circular staircase, her hand fan fluttering in front of her face.

"Yeah, uh, I guess. I kind of got lost and I'm pretty tired and all."

"Well, good for you. Glad to have the company," she said, descending the steps with a very womanly walk. "Why are you just standing there?"

"I was waiting for a drink."

"Well, you gotta ask for one, honey, they don't just come to you!" said Mesmerelda.

"No, uh, the girl was getting one for me."

"Which girl?"

"The one you sent for me?"

"Honey, I hate to burst your bubble but I didn't send any girl out there for you. My girl's don't get here for another few hours at least. What was her name?"

"Milly."

"Sorry, stranger, no Milly here."

Roy thought for a moment, glancing towards the floor.

"Millicent Gifford?"

Mesmerelda went pale as though she swallowed arsenic.

"Roy, honey, ah think ah better get you that drink now."

Six: Milly

Roy sat in a leather chair in the parlour room and in a short moment the wooden doors slid open and Mesmerelda came in carrying a silver tray. On it was a bucket with ice and two crystal glasses, and a forty-ounce bottle of Jack. Mesmerelda poured the golden-brown liquid and it splashed over the ice, which crackled with pleasure.

"There you go, darlin'," she said, then poured one for herself and sat down, taking a sip.

"So what was so important that you had to serve a stiff drink first?"

"Well," said Mesmerelda, taking another sip of whiskey, "I'm really hopin' it was just some sick joke, but the girl you said brought you here-"

"Millicent Gifford."

"Yes. Well, she's been dead going on fifty years!"

Roy took a sip of his whiskey. Then another.

"Look, I'm sorry, honey, it's probably all just some sick little joke someone was playin' on a stranger. It's just that there's very little history to this town and that's one of the few black marks we've got and the folks round here take it all too seriously." She guzzled down the last of her Jack and filled the glass again with a double shot.

Roy felt that creepy feeling come over him again, and he tried to concentrate and ignore the heat and the morbid strangeness of this empty dead town. He tried to fight off this hovering sense of confusion, of why he couldn't seem to get out of here.

"Wait a minute," said Roy, his voice getting a bit aggressive. "When I was on the front porch a few hours ago. Someone creaked open the door and you shouted, 'Close that darn door, Milly!'"

"Yeah, I certainly did," said Mesmerelda. "See, Millicent Gifford was a sweet young girl killed at her senior prom back in the late fifties by a serial killer. She was pretty, popular, and every guy would have died-or killed-to be with her. And everyone in Lebanon Junction,

43

Kentucky loved her. It's said that her ghost still wanders the town." She

took a gulp of whiskey. "So whenever someone creeps around or is

caught spyin' or somethin' the saying goes is to tell Milly to get away.

Her ghost, you know? Lebanon Junction's got it's ghosts like any other

town. The girl you saw was Violet. She was doing some cleanin up and

stuff. I sent her out for groceries so she'll be back shortly."

"Mesmerelda, do you think that Violet-"

"No! Oh no!" said Mesmerelda, cutting him off. "Violet would

never, never, do such a horrid thing!" She filled her glass with more

whiskey and gulped it down. "I'm sorry, I'm just being an old fool. A

silly, drunk old fool."

"Well, I didn't mean..."

"Oh, no, now you don't apologize. Don't you even dare. I'm

reacting like this cause of myself. Would you like some more whiskey,

darlin'?"

"Sure."

"See," said Mesmerelda, leaning over and tilting the whiskey

bottle to pour, "-and I caution I might be dating myself by telling you

this-I went to high school with Millicent Gifford. In fact I was even at the prom where she was killed. Even more to the fact, I was friends with her.

"We were all dancing around and somebody found her body and came running into the gym. It was a guy and girl, and I think they went to their car to make out. The girl comes in all hysterical and the guys ranting and drags everyone outside. Well, when I finally caught a clue on what was going on I pushed my way to the front and saw Milly's body lying there and her throat was torn clean open like some wild animal had got to her, a fox or something. The worst part about it was her eyes. They was open and in shock and all glassy, kind of like when someone's about to cry."

"That's terrible, finding your friend dead at the prom like that. What'd you guys do?"

"Well, needless to say that sort of killed the rest of the prom," said Mesmerelda, her southern charm still striving through her sadness.

"No, I mean the police, the body, what happened. Did they catch the son of a bitch?"

"Yeah. Yeah, they caught the guy. Very next day in fact. Milly was supposed to go the prom with a guy named Ray McMickle. Ray was your total all American, tall, handsome, great future. Wouldn't have stayed in this town, nuh uh. About two months before school ended, Ray disappeared. People caught glimpses of him on the streets, just as he rounded a corner. But nobody could catch him. It was like the guy was mist or something. So obviously everyone was on the lookout for this guy. The town had loved him almost as much as Milly. But Ray had not only disappeared, he'd snapped. He went on a two month long killing spree that ended with Milly's body at the prom. From then on the town of Lebanon Junction, Kentucky, became famous for being the hometown of Ray McMickle, one of the most notorious serial killers the south has ever known." Mesmerelda sipped her whiskey.

Roy inhaled deeply and drank with her. He was starting to feel the effects of the whiskey, which made him forget the effects of the heat. And the house felt cooler as the sun had begun to set.

"Y'know, I like this room. It's cozy. What kind of wood is this?"

"Cherry mahogany," said Mesmerelda. "So put a coaster under your drink."

"The parlour, huh?"

"Nah, this is kind of my office. The girls entertain in the next room and there's a powder room in the back where they prepare themselves. They can come in discreetly through the back door. Speaking of which, I'll get you a room for the night. Half price on account of all the trouble, just so you know southern hospitality ain't dead."

"About that," said Roy, thinking to himself how thankful he was that the topic of serial killers had been averted, "I just sort of ended up here cause I got lost on my way to getting lost, if you know what I mean. I don't want a piece of whatever it is that goes on here."

"Well, darlin', if it's gettin' lost you want then Lebanon Junction, Kentucky is the best place for you! You know we're the town farthest from any other town in America? Just stay away from the parlour and the girls won't bother you. If you have to come down for a drink, the kitchen's on the left, the parlour's on the right. Got it?"

"Got it."

Roy picked up his bag and waited for Mesmerelda to rise and show him to his room. But she still sat there, giving him this strangely suspicious look.

"Roy," she said, putting down her drink, each little movement oh so feminine despite her age. "What's your last name?"

Roy froze and looked at her.

"Why," he stated.

"Just curious," she said. Roy delayed his answer and dragged out his pause a lot longer than he should have, judging by the look of discomfort on Mesmerelda's alcoholically sweaty face.

"Stanich."

Mesmerelda held his gaze, hers cold and stoic. Then she burst out laughing, her head flung back and she was flailing about as though she were a giddy teenage schoolgirl again. Roy stood there and tried to force a smile but he didn't share her joke.

"I'm sorry," said Mesmerelda, laughing through tears. Roy shook his head slightly and then rubbed the back of his neck as though to relieve his frustration.

"So you mean to tell me that you thought I was some sort of reincarnation of the serial killer Ray McMickle come back to terrorize the town?"

"Yes," said Mesmerelda, snorting and nodding her head. "I'm sorry Roy, this whole thing is silly. It was that Ghost of Milly Gifford thing, it makes me crazy. I should never have started on these southern tales of terror. Those are best left for Hallowe'en. C'mon, I'll show you to your room."

<u>Seven: This Town Doesn't Blow, It Sucks</u>

Mesmerelda had left Roy to himself in his room and told him just to relax and that Violet would bring him up some fresh towels.

"If you need anything just sneak on down to the kitchen and help yourself. You might hear some noise and all but it shouldn't be too bad."

"Thanks," said Roy. "Hey, Mesmerelda?"

"Yes, darlin'?"

"Do you still have a picture of Milly Gifford? Just so I can see."

Mesmerelda thought for a moment then said, "Certainly. It might just take me a moment to dig it up, but I'll leave it on the table in the front lobby if I can find it."

He took a tour of the room, slow lazy steps around the bed, his hands running over the wine-coloured curtains and his eyes admiring the quaint four poster bed. He poked his head into the bathroom to check it out then decided to take a cold shower before bed so he could cool off and clear his head.

Roy got undressed and found some courtesy soap and shampoo and went into the shower, making the water just cool enough to feel a frigid sting, lathered himself up.

He was washing his hair and even though he leaned back his head he still managed to get shampoo in his eyes, enough to smart and blind him. He stopped suddenly because he heard a noise.

"It's like the freaking shower scene in Psycho," he muttered to himself. "Hello?" he called, poking his head out of the curtain. No answer. Another thunking sound came from outside the bathroom door.

"What the fuck," he said quietly, letting himself hear his own voice purely for his own reassurance. He put a foot on the floor and was about to step out of the shower when the door to the bathroom opened. Roy's heart jumped around in his chest and he nearly slipped on the floor because the intruder startled him.

"Mr. Stanich?" said the girl in her southern drawl. Roy nearly ripped down the shower curtain trying to hang on to it and he could barely see with the shampoo in his eyes.

"You scared the fuck out of me," he said.

"Oh my God, ah'm sorry, Mr. Stanich, ah didn't hear the shower goin'. Ah'm Violet," she said. Roy began to try and wipe the shampoo out of his eyes but being a little nervous at having been caught off-guard he wasn't having much luck. "Ah know you didn't wanna be bothered Mr. Stanich, but ah just brought you some towels like Mesmerelda said. Just in time too, you're gonna kill yourself on the floor. Lift up your foot."

He did and she arranged one of the towels on the floor to give him some grip on the floor.

"Ah'll just leave the rest on the edge of the sink here for you," she said as she looked up from her knees.

"Oh. Oh thanks, thanks a lot," said Roy, his eyes still stinging. He couldn't really get a look at her no matter how much he squinted but from the sound of her voice she was quite pretty.

"Um, Mr. Stanich," said Violet. "you can step back in the shower now. Ah feel like ah'm talking into a microphone."

"Ah. Sorry," said Roy and he pulled himself back into the shower.

"Ah'll just let myself out Mr. Stanich. Sorry to have disturbed you," said Violet, and Roy could tell by her outline that she was giving him a lingering look back over her shoulder. The door clicked shut and he finished his shower.

Roy put on a pair of boxer shorts and flopped down on the bed with the Guns & Rifle magazine that had been thoughtfully left on the bedside table. It had already darkened and there was a slight din from the parlour downstairs, men laughing and girls giggling. From time to time Roy heard footsteps stomping up the stairs and a door slamming but the walls here were quite thick and he heard very little else.

He was just grateful for the darkness and the fact that the air had cooled down to a reasonable temperature. That, and he was still damp from the shower so he felt a lot more comfortable. Another slug of whiskey would go well but he couldn't be bothered getting up and going downstairs. He didn't want to run into any people. Might as well just stay anonymous and unseen. Easier to get lost that way.

He nearly fell asleep once or twice, but was woken by a rousing, rowdy rise in the level of the volume from downstairs. He tried to picture what it was caused by: a man winning big at a small time craps table; a girl jiggling her breasts for the amusement of the drunken crowd.

This is all too corny, Roy thought to himself. *Trapped in a Kentucky whorehouse in a small town and all those sounds from downstairs like they were out of some B-rated film written by some hack writer who should've been out scoring babes instead of agonizing over words in the dead of night.*

He took the now crushed copy of Guns & Rifle magazine and put it back on the counter. He was lying face up on the bed, feeling the thick comforter beneath his back. He put one hand behind his head and stared at the ornate little light fixture above him. He tried to remember why it was he'd left Winnipeg, why it was he was trying to go to Meridian, Mississippi, and why he'd even bothered to follow the luscious red-head off the bus, which had seemed to unravel it all. It wasn't so much the fact that the din from downstairs had faded then the fact that Roy had drifted off to sleep, the little smile upon his face a possible indication he was actually looking forward to morning.

Dreamless sleeps were the worst. Because one never knew if they'd slept or what had happened to their mind during that time. Had it been stolen? Had it died until sunrise? The night was full of questions because no one could possibly see anything for what it was in the dark.

Roy lay sprawled upon his back, his arms and legs akimbo as he experienced just such a dreamless sleep. Dreamless sleep never solved anything because without dreams there was nothing to be desired when awake, and nothing to be accomplished.

But they were oh so relaxing. So when Roy heard the lock to the door to his room making the same thunk-albeit a muffled one-as he'd heard in the shower, he was quite helpless to do anything about it. He just lay there as though a dream had come to visit him, but he knew without a doubt in his sleep-laden, dead weight mind that this was no dream. It was just that his body was unable to do anything, though he began to have the desire to move.

Clearly he heard it: the door slide open, the careful, quiet steps into the room, the door closing with but a whisper of a creek. Roy still felt the dampness of the shower but now it had become a cold sweat. His skin felt as though he was slowly sinking into snow.

And a hot hand gripped his heart to still it's beating when he felt the gentle touch on his legs as they were pushed apart. He was finally able to pull himself a little ways out of the dreamless sleep. Just enough to think a bit and utter a word.

"Violet?"

But he wasn't awake enough to wonder why he had said that. Was it because Violet had given him that lingering last look, as he stood naked in the shower? Was it because he'd had to use all his will power to stop her sweet southern voice from giving him blood sausage?

Roy could finally hear himself breathing now, heavier. And someone else's breath down near his knees.

"MMMmmmmmmmmmmmmmmm," said Roy, his mouth breaking into a slight smile. He was trying to say the name but he couldn't. Perhaps because he wanted it too much, he couldn't say her name. Mmmmmmmmmmmmmmesmerelda, but it wouldn't come out when he tried again. Just: MMMMMmmmmmmmmmmmmmmm.

And so what if she was, like, seventy years old? He knew from that whiskey drenched voice of hers that she had a seething, steaming snatch beneath her skirts just ready to go.

"Would you like your Jack Daniels on the rocks, darlin'?" he imagined her saying, pouring the syrupy brown liquid over her breasts in such a southern faux pas.

Lips were already kissing his and he imagined they were Mesmerelda's all covered, sticky, slippery, and hot with alcohol.

Oh I'd pour it all over your lips, baby, spread your legs and I'll pour it all over your lips and lick every inch of that red little rose of yours.

He felt himself get lighter. The lips left his. There was no more weight upon his body. He tried to turn and twist so he could see who had come into his room, but as soon as he moved he felt his legs thrust apart again, held there by strong hands. Mesmerelda was certainly skilled in her talents. Roy felt his eyes slowly opening against the fugue but a hand kept his head pushed sideways into the bed.

"MMMmmmmmmmmmmmm," he said again, still unable to form words. Hands left his legs and began to remove his underwear, tearing them off with a slow ripping sound. A cool wet tongue slithered up his thigh and Roy felt that he was able to move his head again. The hands held down his hips as the tongue neared his throbbing penis. He lifted his head, struggling against its dead weight, to have a look at the succulent lips that he now felt near to him, breathing on him, making him very, very hard. He couldn't make out the face at first because his stiff cock jutting through it blocked it, bisecting it. His eyes took a moment to adjust to the darkness, and the black face rose above his sex as though it were a shark, and the mouth opened wide to claim it.

"MMMMMmmmmmmm," said Roy, and the mouth was threateningly close to his cock, the breath hot, the damp vapour of the saliva making the tip of him the just slightest bit wet, and the face became visible in the darkness.

Pig tails.

"Mmmmmmmmmmmmiiiiilllllly?"

"Sssssshhhhh, quiet darlin'," she said, her lips smacking together from the wetness. "Just relax."

"No, I..." said Roy, his body tensing up a little from nervousness and confusion. He tried to lift himself up but couldn't. "You're dead, Milly."

But he distinctly felt her hands on his thighs, he felt her wet, warm breath at the tip of his penis.

"Just relax," she said again. "Let me take care of you." Her voice alone was enough to intoxicate him and it put him back down on the bed."

"I didn't want this tonight. I didn't want a girl. I don't want a dead girl."

"Ah can take care of you, Roy. Ah can make you happy," she said, and he finally felt her mouth descend upon his cock, the soft, wet lips closing upon the head. Roy closed his eyes and sighed with pleasure. He felt the lips slide down the shaft of his penis until they reached the base, and then they slowly came back up again, leaving little trails of spittle that clung to his skin.

Milly went slowly up and down his shaft, again and again, her tongue putting pleasurable pressure each time she ascended him. Her hands rubbed his thighs and hips skillfully. Then she took him deeply one more time before she lifted herself up and let his phallus fall from her mouth.

Roy looked up, disappointed from the somewhat sudden absence of pleasure, but all he could see were Milly's breasts bursting from the tightly knotted top she wore, his cock superimposed over her cleavage. All he wanted to do was lie her on the bed and stick his cock in her cleavage and rub it back and forth until he came all over her tits.

But Milly wasn't finished. She'd only taken a moment to catch her breath (if ghosts did indeed have breath) and again her head plunged down in a slow and tantalizing swoon.

Her lips kissed his balls, and she pushed at the soft, folding flesh with her tongue, pushing it upwards until she got underneath it. She used all the force she possibly could as she slathered her tongue in that sensitive spot. She took one of her hands and grabbed hold of his cock, rubbing the underside of it with her thumb while her fingers massaged the head.

Roy moaned, "Oh fuck, oh yes, God yes," and grabbed hold of the bed sheets beneath him, clenching them in his fists. Milly's tongue and lips slapped and smacked their way back up to his balls and all over them and then to his cock again, her hand now gripping him so tightly as to hold in Roy's now imminent explosion. He felt her tongue making figure eights around the base of his cock as it worked its way back up to the head, then she swallowed him whole again, her hand working up and down with her mouth, coaxing, drawing upon the well.

Her motions became vigorous now, her lips and tongue and hand applying significant pressure, and Roy's penis gave with a spasm

Steve Zinger

in Milly's mouth. She felt the urgency and moved even faster along his shaft, and Roy's entire body tensed with the anticipation of the ultimate shudder of pleasure. Milly felt another throb in her mouth and the hard penis reverberated as the pipes within filled up in the moment before completion and the muscles all around the area tensed, ready to force everything out, awaiting one last lick of the tongue.

Milly opened her mouth for one moment, breaking contact with the quivering member in the last second before the milk boiled over. Roy's hips immediately became eager and began to rise off the bed as his thing begged to be eaten. And, as though it had a mind of its own, as though it knew the exact moment when Milly's ghostly lips would touch it once more, it exploded. Her hungry mouth clamped upon it once more, the warm liquid hitting the roof of her mouth and making it sticky and white until she swallowed up his sugar, gently stroking and coaxing every last drop out.

Roy relaxed his muscles and dropped back down to the bed, letting out several heavy breaths. His hands relaxed their grip upon the bed sheets and his head lolled to the side as he felt himself in desire of sleep, dreamless or not. But he also wanted to look once more at Milly, the ghost who was sucking his dick, and then he'd noticed that the sucking had slowly faded away until he felt nothing. He lifted his head and looked down the end of the bed and saw only a black mass of shadow between his legs-

-The doorway open, filled with fire, Mesmerelda standing there, her red hair alive and angry, her eyes hollow pits and her mouth open with long, long fangs, oh so white-

Roy snapped up, the image burned in his mind as though someone had forced it under his skin with a needle, his body cold and smelly with sweat. The door was closed. The room was still and dark and quiet but for the eerie and pleasant chirping of a cricket. He tried to tell himself it was just a dream but he looked down and saw himself sticky and naked, his underwear torn in half beneath him.

Eight: The Fluttering of Wings

Roy got up and found some fresh clothes from his bag, just a plain grey T-shirt and some boxer shorts, and he opened his door. Everything was quiet and fairly dark and he guessed it was somewhere after 3am. Most of the doors to the bedrooms around him were open, a sure sign they were unoccupied given the type of place he was in.

He walked slowly in the hallway so as not to bump into anything in the dark. He felt much like an intruder and looked like one from the kind of steps he took.

There was one door that was closed and Roy put his ear to it, about to knock. Mesmerelda's room, perhaps, but he couldn't be certain. He withheld his hand at the last moment because of the sounds of fucking he heard from inside. If it was Mesmerelda there wouldn't be much point in disturbing her anyway. So he continued on and went towards the stairs.

The atmosphere of the whole house had become eerie and saturnine and Roy crept down the stairs as though a man walking to his death, resigned to his fate. He looked into the parlour and the sitting room where he'd drank whiskey with his hostess. Empty.

The heat had finally lifted and left the house cold, but Roy knew that another onslaught was being prepared for the next day. His spine was sweaty and cold and Roy took a deep breath, enjoying the invigorating chill of the still air all around him.

He saw a pack of cigarettes on a table beneath the front window and he took one and lit it.

"I can't fucking sleep," he muttered as he looked out the window at the pitch-black miasma of dusty road and twisted trees.

"Why don't ya'll go outside and take a walk?" said Milly. Roy kept his gaze fixed upon the window, his body unnerved and stoic.

"There's nothing out there," he said. His arms were folded and he lifted one to put the cigarette to his mouth. "Just emptiness. Death and darkness."

"Look closer. Ya'll ain't lookin' hard enough," said Milly. Roy caught a glimpse of her out of the corner of his eye: Blond hair in pig tails, her button-down shirt knotted up between her breasts, cut off jeans shorts that showed every inch of her thigh. "You keep running away from nothing and all you keep goin' to is nothing."

Roy let the smoke filter out between his lips and caress his nose and sting his eyes.

"Yeah, but where would I go, anyway?"

Silence. He spun around after a moment, startled not by the presence of the ghost of Millicent Gifford but by it's sudden absence. He felt his heart thumping away in his chest, but that was a good thing, he thought, even though he felt a certain kind of fear that was like a gentle ripple on a calm lake.

Roy turned back to the black window and through his insomnia stared outside, whispered, "But where to go," and his gaze drifted down the road to what was the opposite direction, that unnamed way that the street sign didn't bother to point out.

He slipped on some shoes and went outside in only his T-shirt and boxer shorts and his only light was the little heater of his cigarette.

The only sound were his feet kicking up dirt on the unpaved road. To his right the trees loomed over him with a quiet green menace. He came to the street sign:

(Blank)

75 miles

He tried to make out the words that looked as though they'd been scratched off by years of weather. He squinted in the dark, then pulled out his lighter and squinted further. Looked like...next town? That certainly didn't help much, he-

-Looked quickly to his left. What the fuck was that? Something there. Only the trees fluttering and waving their branches up and down, and Roy snapped off the lighter quickly because it was getting hot enough to burn his hand. He took a deep breath to relax and then sucked on the last of his cigarette and flung it away.

He walked the unnamed way but it was only moments that he slowed his steps because even an awful dirt road wasn't this bad and it seemed as though it just faded away and when he looked as far ahead as he could he saw pretty much nothing but a thickening of trees and still nowhere to go and-

67

"Hey, baby, you made it!"

He had to turn a bit and he saw, against the pitch green backdrop of the darkened forest the dim glow of Milly's ghost.

"That's what ah do, sometimes, is just walk when ah can't sleep. Clears my head. Is your head clear, Roy?"

"I...hm. I don't know," said Roy, and he forced out a laugh. Milly seemed to ignore him and she turned and walked away. Roy raised his eyebrows in a bit of a worried expression and followed lest he lose her again.

He broke into the forest, thinking he would plunge himself into absolute and utter darkness, but all he had to do was keep his eye on the glimpses of the glow of Milly's ghost. He weaved after her through the trees, only tripping up once or twice. His breath became heavy from the light run trying to catch her, and the leaves on the forest floor crunched beneath his feet.

The ghostly glow disappeared from his view and Roy chased it further, then doubled back and did circles and went helter skelter around the bush but couldn't find any sign of it. He put his hand on the trunk of a tree and bent over while he tried to catch his breath, his lungs expelling the tar from the tobacco.

He took many deep breaths trying to regain his wind.

"This is where he did it," said Milly. She was so cute in her skimpy outfit, and even though Roy saw fingers of sadness creeping over her face there was still a lightness to her being. The kind of thing that would draw people to her so they could share it. "Ah was takin' a walk before the prom to clear my head. Ah was pretty upset because ah didn't have a date. He'd up and snapped and just left and then all the bodies started disappearin'."

"Who..." said Roy.

"Ray McMickle. The school was just about a half-hour walk from the road there so ah figured ah would just come here and take a few minutes and clear my head. Well, my head was just floatin' with the fact that ah was stood up an I felt terrible for feelin' terrible cause all them people had died. But a part of me was tryin' to be happy cause I was in a beautiful white chiffon dress, all frilly and lacy, and the forest was comin' alive again cause it was spring and I spun around and...

"...there he was..."

She spun around and lifted her hand in a gesture not unlike that of a model presenting new merchandise; but she was more like a gloomy pantomime. If ghosts had tears she would have cried.

"Milly..." said Roy, and he felt her pain. Oh God, why? he thought? Why am I feeling this as though it was happening to me? Was it because ghosts don't have souls and they had to transmit their pain to those they were haunting to shed themselves of it, if only for a night? Did Milly's soul still feel the torment of her death even after all these years? "Tell me..."

He shook as the words left his lips. He would take her pain upon himself, here in the darkness of the forest.

"His eyes were ringed in black as though he'd rubbed them with coal. He looked like he hadn't slept in a month. So ah stopped and looked at him. Of course ah was a little surprised to see him. No one had in months. Half his face looked like a shadow because he hadn't been shaving regularly. Ah...ah didn't know what to do, or say. Ah just kind of stood there and ah tried to smile like ah always did but ah could feel it fadin' like the sun was. Ah was out in the middle of the forest where no one could hear me and the sun was going down faster than it ever did.

"Ah heard the branches crunch and ah realized he was comin' closer to me. He had a knife in his hand, Roy. He looked like shit. Sweaty an' just plain crazy! That knife was six inches long and he told me he wanted to stick it in me. And ah couldn't move, Roy. Ah felt like ah was underwater."

Roy leaned up against a tree trunk, trying to find some solace and security among the darkness and the monstrous, ominous overhanging branches.

"He pulled my hair so hard my arms sprung outwards and my back felt like it would break. My neck felt so vulnerable and cold and he took his knife an pressed the edge of the blade to my skin. He..."

Milly put her dead hands to her face.

"He cut my throat, Roy!" she cried. "Ah felt my own blood trickling down my neck to my shoulders and down to my chest. He got drops of blood on my white dress. You don't know what it's like to feel your own life draining out a you like a river. It's especially worse when you can't even see it. You got to imagine it, you got to imagine what's happening to yourself.

"And then he clamped his lips to my neck. He sucked and bit at my wound like some stark raving animal and I felt it in my fingertips, Roy, ah felt myself dying. Ah never pictured myself getting killed but ah somehow always thought ah would scream. But ah couldn't even do that. It was so simple. Dying ah mean. So simple. And that thought brought me to my grave so scared."

Roy closed his eyes. His whole body felt cold, yet serene, and he felt moisture behind his closed lids. Everything was quiet but for the intermittent chirping of a cricket. He slowly opened his eyes, expecting to see Milly gone again, but she was still there, although her glow had faded sorrowfully to nothingness.

She knelt on the ground, her dead fingers digging into the dirt as though her own grave was beneath their very feet and she was somehow barred from it. She moved so Roy could see her neck, the part of her neck that was cut open, but it was so perfect and white and smooth now, preserved in death. But he could tell that Milly still carried the pain of the wound and was still tormented in her own personal Hell by it. He could tell because he heard sounds. Breathing. Quiet, ragged, raspy breaths, windpipe torn and skin shorn, air escaping healthy young lungs.

Roy moved closer to where Milly was, to where she'd told her story. He bent down and put his fingers to the ground like she did, feeling the dirt and the branches and the leaves.

"Milly died here," he said, as though he were alone. He looked up and was face to face with the ghost, inches from that glow.

"Milly didn't die here, Roy," she said. "This was just where the bloodletting took place. Ah had barely any breath left in my body, barely any blood. Ah was in a swoon. Fallin' to the ground and even though his arm was behind my back, ah could barely feel his arm holding me. He picked me up and my equilibrium just swung back and forth. The sun had just set and he carried me away from here..."

"Where..." said Roy, hesitantly, "where did he take you?"

"Where he was supposed to take me that night. He took me to the prom."

Why the hell would he do such a stupid thing like that? thought Roy. For a moment he relaxed and his face had an expression of severe misunderstanding.

"He carried me to his pick-up and put me in the seat beside him," Milly answered, as though reading Roy's thoughts. "He didn't care that I was bleeding all over it. He pulled his pick-up into the parking lot of the school and then laid me out in the flat bed."

Milly dug her fingers further into the dirt.

"He wanted to fuck me, Roy. He wanted to fuck me while ah was bleeding and dying."

"Oh dear God," Roy whispered, the words barely audible on the cold breath coming out from his lips.

"Suck at my neck," she said. She held his gaze and put her hand to her neck, where the wound was first gashed open. As soon as she touched it her eyes became hollow black pits and her body seemed to freeze in that position. Roy was afraid, afraid of the dense green silence of the forest at night, afraid of seeing a man with a five o'clock shadow and a six inch knife come stepping out from between the trees;

74

afraid of touching the ghost of Millicent Gifford as it knelt before him with dead black eyes.

He leaned forward to touch her-and fell over onto the ground. When he picked his head up Milly was nowhere to be seen and Roy's head throbbed as though he'd just woken from a long, cold sleep. He was lying on his stomach on the ground and could feel the branches sticking into him and all the leaves and dirt clinging to his body.

"Milly?" he said, and he was questioning not only her presence in the forest but her existence-whether she had actually been there in the first place. Right now he had only crickets and his own breathing.

And an intermittent crunch of footsteps.

"Oh fuck, what was that," said Roy, pushing himself up on his arms. He felt so naked standing by himself in the middle of the open night air, black nothing forest, no ghost to make like mommy as she suckled him to bring him comfort. He was a sitting duck lying on the ground but at least he felt safe in Mother's arms.

"What the fuck *is* that," said Roy again after hearing some more crunch crunching of branches. He said it louder, as though speaking would keep him grounded, as though sound would melt his fear away like the heat of the rising sun.

The crunch still came every other second or so and tried to picture where it was coming from, but each time he turned to it, it seemed to come from a different angle. He was staggering backwards now, footing shaky on the litter of the forest floor.

"Oh, fuck, he's here, Milly!" screamed Roy. He stepped backwards, bumping into a tree and nearly falling, trying to escape. "Why the fuck did you bring me here?"

He turned and ran from the spot, blindly through the wicked, wizened branches of the dank, dark forest. He didn't turn around but he pictured misty white ghosts chasing him through the branches from above, glinting steel blades flashing fiery silver from beside him, his blood dripping shiny, bubbly red as the hot blades quickly sliced his skin as though it were soft bread.

After a while he stopped running but kept walking, breathing heavily, his arms wrapped around his chest as though trying to keep his heart from exploding. His eyes searched the darkness ahead of him trying to see a way out, to spot the main road.

-Heard the crunching feet-

"Oh fucking Hell!" cried Roy, as though it were an involuntary reflex, simply to swear. He resumed his run, weaving around tree trunks and ducking branches like wrinkled arms that were reaching down trying to snatch at the ends of his shirt as he narrowly dodged them. He switched his path, making a sudden turn in hopes of confusing his pursuer. Stopped behind a tree for a sec.

-Heard the crunching feet-

He pushed himself away from the tree and ran in another direction, this time looking back, trying to get a glimpse of his assailant. Only the darkness was behind him as it was before him, his only demons the sinister shapes of the trees all twisted and hunched, looming all around him. Stopped again, lungs labouring each and every breath, and each and every breath audible. Was he being followed by the very sound of his own breath?

-Feet cracking branches from over there!-

Roy spun. The sound had come from a completely different direction than before. Had he come full circle? Was he now trapped in the forest as he'd been trapped in the town? And each time it was a piece of pussy that had lured him to his fate.

Roy had become too tired to run and now he just backed away from the sound, and each time the sound came from a different direction he bounced to a different one himself. He moved in a spirograph pattern criss-crossing over his own paths several times.

"Oh shit, oh fuck, Milly, he's here," he said, his voice choking with the sorrow of his own impending death. "Why the hell did you bring me here, Milly?"

Roy put his back up against a tree trunk and listened, his head making sudden, jerky movements at every little noise and every little trick his eyes played on him. He heard the crunching from more than one direction now, and he pressed his back so hard into the tree he felt his skin being scratched off through his shirt.

Something touched his shoulder. Roy didn't hesitate, he just screamed and screamed and ran and ran.

Through some sweet mercy of fate, the forest gurbled and coughed up Roy as though it had been given indigestion. Had he not been so drunk and depleted from fear and exhaustion he would have certainly had a mild sense of surprise at having finally found the road.

He staggered out, his body bent double, and he held his stomach. He tasted bile rising in the back of his throat and felt his heart get hot, and he could smell the liquid welling up in him, the fear pushing nausea through his body, making his throat muscles constrict involuntarily.

"I am totally losing my mind," said Roy, trying to force himself to belch so he could hopefully feel some relief in his stomach. With each one he forced out he tasted the hot and spicy/pungent fluid that burst like a bubble of lava in his throat.

"Fucking Christ," he said, his words so simple and simply profane, but they carried much more with them; they carried his sheer fear and utterly simplistic but effective terror. For he'd never felt so helpless before, trapped in Mother's sensory deprivation tank with one of her unearthly creatures stalking him.

Then he felt it and just couldn't help it, and he heaved a pile of vomit at the road, spilling out relief, anger, sadness and stench all at once. He coughed up some more once or twice before he finally stood up and began to walk. He walked slowly as though he'd just been released from the hospital and had not fully recovered his injuries.

But it wasn't back to the great grey whorehouse that Roy went. To him that place was somehow scarred, haunted and he felt the windows looking at him with scorn. Roy's head and his whole body throbbed with the trauma of bringing up everything in his stomach, with his haunted sleep and furious run from his own nightmares. But he had some clarity in his mind now that he wasn't threatened with any sort of fear and he began to think as he walked down the main street of the town of nowhere, Lebanon Junction, Kentucky.

There was actually a serenity to the cool dark night. Deep, utter emptiness of blackened sky with only twinkling white specks letting you know some sort of space was there. He felt no fear now but he felt as though eyes were upon him, other than those of the stars.

He was in front of the door to Scooter's bar now, and he knocked lightly.

"Scooter?" he called, quietly, but still louder than he'd wished to. "It's me. Roy. Can you open up?"

No answer. And why would there be, this late at night? How could he expect anyone to be there? How could he-

"Scooter?"

-expect it at all. Footsteps.

"Scooter? I can here you walking."

When it is night-

Shuffling of feet.

"Open the door please?"

-and one is talking to oneself-

Definite movement.

"I'm all alone out here, Scooter."

-and one is utterly alone-

He is in there.

"Please open the door?"

-one's voice sounds...in the silence so loud-

But why won't he answer?

"Why won't you answer me?"

-one must shudder to wonder if that knock was the one on death's door.

"Fuck," muttered Roy, dejected. He threw his hands at the ground and hung his head in frustration. Took some lazy steps away from the door of the bar. "I've lost myself in some wicked form of reality. Just totally lost. I think I'm lost in my head. I must be lost in my head. Because if I really am lost here, I think I will just go insane."

So lost in his limbo, wrapped up in depressed hang-headedness looking at the ground, he didn't hear the sound. (At first.) Quiet rumbling, rubber popping and crunching pebbles and dust, then sudden bright lights ripping his gaze awake, making his heart beat louder than the crickets chirp in the night. Startled stop and Roy had to brace his balance by stiffening and spreading his arms a bit. And distracted from behind because the door he'd knocked upon (to no avail) had issued forth a Hollywood creek and, though he always said it would never ever scare him, no, not him certainly, he felt a shiver run up and down his back like an angry rat chewing at his spine.

Beginning to turn, he was, but it cocked (cha-chunk) and the big man in the light brown uniform with his dark brown hat and the headlights behind him and the gun in his hand had frozen him once more. The barrel was pointed at him.

But he'd caught a glimpse, he did, and he heard the noise. Thought it was the fluttering of wings, and it was, at first. Then became a furious beat, like that of the angry Satanic heart held high in the hand of the malevolently grinning priest.

And a great shadow descended from overtop of Roy, consuming him totally. He couldn't see, the darkness total absence of light, of sight, and the white lights blinding him utterly. Then a bright orange flash, brighter than the white, and a sound so loud it deafened him, making his ears pop as though in a vacuum, and he felt as though his brain were sucked into nothingness, all his senses voided.

Then it was Black.

Nine: Coca-Cola and Jack Daniel's

Roy woke up with stripes on his face. Some were dark. Some were light. His throat was parched and he stank of the sweat he'd gained from the previous night. But it was the stripes on his face that really bothered him. He picked himself up off the mattress.

Jail cell.

How the hell did I end up in a jail cell? he thought. His body ached, joints creaking from the frosty night before.

"Well, boy, ah see you're up finally."

Roy looked up, rubbing his stiff neck as he did. Deputy Kuthrow sat at a nearby desk with his coffee, staring from behind big smoked glasses at him. Then Roy's memories flooded back.

"You bastard," he said. "You shot Scooter."

84

"Ah'd watch what you'd say, son," said the deputy, taking his feet off the desk. He squared his shoulders, becoming more defensive. "Ah've already got you behind bars, ah can put a bullet in your back if ah want. This ain't Canada you know."

Roy took a deep breath, trying to relax. He was in a very poor position to engage in aggressive negotiations. He ran his fingers through his hair.

"What's it going to take to get me out of here," he said, his voice flat.

"That's where you're lucky, boy. Mesmerelda called last night looking for you. She'll be on shortly to get you."

"Do you care to explain," said Roy, giving the deputy a harsh, hard stare from under his dark eyebrows, "why you whizzed a bullet by my head last night?"

"You should be thanking me, you little shit. There was a wild wolf come jumping up from behind you. Dangerous to stay out that late at night. These parts, that is..."

Roy could tell Deputy Kuthrow had a faraway look in his eyes even though he had his sunglasses on. He was thinking, contemplating on something. He looked back at Roy, who had a look that clearly stated disbelief. Deputy Kuthrow read his expression as though reading his mind.

"You think ah'm a liar, do you?" he said, stunned that anyone would dare challenge him. He walked up to the bars of the cell, so close his nose had crossed the threshold.

"Boy, if you wanna take me on ah'll put you down faster than a two dollar whore." The beauty about Deputy Kuthrow was that he was a man who filled his profanity with the utmost conviction.

Luckily for Roy, he didn't get a chance to test his mettle in the smoked-glass stare of the deputy's glasses and uniformed broad shoulders. Mesmerelda had arrived.

"Deputy Kuthrow," said Mesmerelda in her southern twang. "How do? Ah trust ya'll've been keeping are guest in good spirits?"

"Ah want this boy out of here. You got that?"

"Now, now, Deputy," said Mesmerelda, "let's show our guest some southern charm. Do remember ah was in the hospitality business before you were even in diapers."

"Just cut his bail and get him the hell out of my sight."

Mesmerelda opened her hand purse and peeked into it for a moment. Roy took a good look at her face and studied the few wrinkles she had scrunched around her eyes.

Mesmerelda put her hand to her cheek in a dainty gesture and said, "Deputy, ah'm afraid a barely have a dime on me. Ah certainly have enough to buy are guest a beverage on the walk home, but ah'll have to owe you on the bail if you don't mind."

The deputy's expression changed not a bit.

"You come by the house sometime. Ah'll comp you room, food and board."

She ran her long nailed finger across his cheek and he stood there as though he were stone. Then he came to life and walked over to Roy's cell and unlocked the door with one of his fifty keys.

"Why thankee, deputy," said Mesmerelda as she curtsied. Roy couldn't help but have his gaze fix upon the deputy's as though it was pulled there by rope. He tried to picture the man's eyes behind the glasses but could barely see anything but only the faintest white with red rims behind the dark lenses. And it was no use challenging the deputy. He'd already fired at him once, certainly a warning shot.

They walked out to a white noon sun and a thick, wet heat.

"Sometimes my womanly charms do come in handy, don'tcha think?" said Mesmerelda.

"He must have been in what passed for a good mood today."

"Let's get you on home before he changes his mind, then. You thirsty?"

"Yeah but it can wait," said Roy. Mesmerelda made a loop of her arm and presented it to Roy, who just gave her back a confused look.

"A man and a woman walk arm in arm in the south," she explained. "Ah may be a bit old fashioned but ah think it's only gentlemanly."

"Well then I'm charmed," said Roy, and he put his arm through hers. She smiled at him and she held her umbrella with the burgundy flower print over their heads to keep off the sun.

"Mesmerelda, are you sure you're over seventy?" asked Roy, sounding a bit like a child.

"Sure as the sun's beating on are backs," she said. "My mama raised me to be a perfectionist when it came to being a lady, so ah kept my looks."

Suddenly Roy stopped. He felt someone looking at him and he turned his head and luckily caught a glimpse of a dirty white T-shirt and scraggly dark hair disappearing around a corner.

"Roy, what is it?" asked Mesmerelda.

"Someone's spying on me," he said, and he unhooked his arm and rushed over to the corner. He rounded it but found, obviously, nothing. Not a trace of a soul. "Someone was here," he said. "Looking at me."

Mesmerelda was just catching up to him, panting heavily.

"C'mon, Roy, it's hot. People imagine things in the heat. Let's just go home and have a drink. It's much cooler in the house."

Roy just stood there, looking down the alleyway.

"Roy, you're starin' at a dumpster."

He looked to his left, away from Mesmerelda, but he saw no one there either. Then he looked back down the alleyway at the dumpster and felt completely silly.

"Yeah. Let's go already," he said, and hooked back onto her arm reluctantly. "Maybe...there were these guys in the bar who didn't take well to me. Maybe it was them following me."

"Roy, stop it already, you're being neurotic for no good reason."

"Reg and Donny-boy. Yeah, that was them. Reg and Donny-boy."

Mesmerelda yanked on his arm and stopped him.

"Reg is a full-blown alcoholic and Donny-boy is just another way of saying mama's boy. Ah wouldn't bother yourself with them cause they're low-lifes." Roy looked right at her and she seemed almost angry with him. "And besides, there was no one there anyway. We would have seen them."

"Yeah. Yeah, okay, maybe you're right. It's the heat getting to me. I didn't see anything. It was the heat."

"That's better," said Mesmerelda, satisfied. She hooked back onto his arm.

And they walked back to the great grey whorehouse together.

"Ah was going to buy you a Coca Cola but you look like you could do more for a stiff shot of Jack Daniel's."

"Thanks," said Roy, still rubbing the stiffness out of his muscles.

"Rocks?"

"Sure."

"Ah'll make it a double, too." She handed him his drink and he drank it down in three gulps, then she refilled his glass, which he sipped.

"How long have I been here, Mesmerelda?"

"'Bout a day, I reckon. Why?"

Roy put down his drink.

"I think I'm losing my mind," he said, and he spread his hands and looked at the backs of them. "Are these my hands?" he whispered.

"Maybe I ought to leave you alone," she said.

"No!" said Roy, his head snapping up as though he'd snapped back from a dream. "I don't want to be alone really. I've been getting very lonely lately."

"Take a sip of your whiskey. Maybe you just have to forget yourself for a while."

"I think that's half the problem. I forgot where I came from. I forgot where I was going. I think I'm forgetting who I am."

"Don't be all silly, now, Roy. You're just going through a rough time."

"Look at me," he said, holding his hands up. "I'm shaking. Still from last night. Like it's dark and cold and I'm all alone and scared."

Mesmerelda took a glass of whiskey and moved closer to Roy. "Just don't think about it," she said, putting a hand lightly on his shoulder. "This is the worst place to feel like you're losin' yerself. This town's dying, Roy, slowly. Don't die with it."

"Then why can't I get out?" he asked, almost pleading to her as though she were his goddess. "I tried three times to get out but I can't. I tried last night to leave but the town tried to drive me nuts. It slowly and quietly put it's arms around me and now it's keeping me here. I'm stuck here."

Mesmerelda just looked at him, a blank, stoic look, completely unwavering. Roy tried to hold her gaze but couldn't, he just dropped his head and forced out a laugh.

"You think I'm crazy, don't you?" he said.

"No, Roy, ah don't think you're crazy."

"Oh, boy," he said, and leaned his head back, putting his hand to his forehead. He looked out the window across the horizon, seeing nothing but dusty roads and forested rolling hills. "I forgot where I was going in the first place."

"Meridian, Mississippi."

"Oh yeah. Right. Why the hell did I decide to go there?"

"Couldn't help you there, Roy."

"I think it just sounded good. And I had to decide on my bus ticket. Or something." He looked out the window and took another swig of whiskey. And wondered what was *there*.

"Mesmerelda," he said. "What's the next town called."

"What?"

"The sign at the end of the road says there's a town seventy-five miles from here. What's it called."

"Oh, well it's called Szjnbdton."

"What?"

"Ah said it's called Szjnbdton."

Roy turned his head and said, "I can't hear you, say it slowly, please."

"Sz...jn...bd...ton."

He stood up and nearly threw his whiskey to the ground and said, "Mesmerelda, I can't fucking hear you!"

"Roy, please, calm down. You're not well. Maybe you should go upstairs and relax."

"Don't tell me what to..." but he stopped himself. He grabbed hold of his head again. "My head feels like it's in a vacuum. My ears feel like they're going to explode."

Mesmerelda went over to him and took his whiskey glass. She put an arm around his shoulder and put the glass to his lips so he could finish off his drink. Then she put down the glass and started to lead him out of the sitting room.

"C'mon, Roy," she said in her sweet southern voice, "you've been up all night, you must be over tired. Ah'll take you upstairs and lie you down."

"Yeah. Yeah, I guess so. I'm not nuts, I'm just really, really tired. Take me upstairs," he said, and she did, listening to him babble all along the way.

"People see things when they're tired, right?" he asked.

"Just lie down, honey," said Mesmerelda, and she pulled back the sheets for him. "Don't worry about it. Ah can get you another whiskey to keep by your bed if you like." She drew the curtains to block out some of the sunlight.

"People hallucinate when they're too tired, right? They hear things? They see things? I don't think I've slept well in two days. The last time I slept was on the bus but that wasn't very good. I was next to this guy who smelled like onions and shit. Who was that man on the street? Deputy wants me to leave but I can't. I saw a bat last night, Mesmerelda. It was going to eat me."

"Roy, you're babbling. Please calm down, just relax. You'll be okay," she said, and she lay down next to him. "You want me to lie with you, baby? Ah'll stay here with you. My God, you're shaking, baby." She had her arms around him and she rocked him slowly back and forth. It was as though he was freezing cold, but he felt warm from the alcohol.

"Keep talking," he whispered. "I need to hear your voice. Please, I don't want to be left alone ever again." Almost in tears now.

"Ssshh, that's okay, baby. Mesmerelda's here. Ah'll stay with you as long as ah have to. Just lie in my arms and have sweet dreams and forget everything else, baby darlin'."

He was cold and rocking back and forth and he felt her warm lips kiss his forehead gently as he was sucked into sleep, another black abyss from which there was no turning back.

Ten: Animal Husbandry

It felt like people were fucking me. Even in my dreams they were fucking me. And I couldn't help it. I couldn't help anything anymore because I was stuck. My arms were pulled to their lengths and held down, and my legs were spread wide until it felt my knees would splinter. I was totally helpless.

I knew I had fallen asleep in Mesmerelda's arms and I had to wonder if I was having this dream because she had decided to take advantage of me while I had no other choice in the matter; while I was slipping into madness and the darkness of sleep from which there was no return.

My arms and legs were splayed out as though I was waiting for someone to throw knives at me for a circus side show.

Something wet was milking my cock.

I could only imagine Mesmerelda hanging over me, nothing of her touching me but her wet pussy swallowing my cock, her hands above my shoulders holding herself up and her knees next to my hips making dents in the bed. Her breasts dangling oh so close to my face, the skin near the cleavage just a bit wrinkled from age. And her fiery red hair moving back and forth with each thrust.

But I could only imagine because this was a dream of every sense but sight. No matter which way I looked I could only see the Black.

Then my dreams answered my thoughts and I saw a bit of light. The door to the bedroom; someone was standing in it, a very big man. I was trying to focus. Deputy Kuthrow? The man had wings. Big, black gargoyle wings. The man pointed his sharp, clawed finger at me and I heard him laugh a quiet but very sinister titter.

I felt my throat muscles constricting slowly. He was choking me from afar. Then he allowed me a just a glimpse.

And I saw what was fucking me. It was a bat.

There were wounds at my wrists and I felt them tear open and blood pour out of them like a waterfall, the skin shorn apart in ragged rips.

In the most sensuously grim and raspy voice the man said, "Go find the Black Hand."

Eleven: They're Both History

Roy snapped his head up as though he'd woken and thought he was late for work. He dropped back down from the fatigue and smothered his face with a pillow.

Dear God, I hope that I'm not naked down there, he thought to himself. He looked down. Boxer shorts. What a relief.

Mesmerelda came out of the bathroom with a cup of water and said, "You're awake!" She put the water next to the bed and put her hand to his forehead.

"Were you here the whole time?" he asked.

"Yes, ah was. You must've been having a bad dream or something because you were shaking around a bit."

"I was dreaming that someone had cut open my wrists and was bleeding me to death," said Roy.

"Well, that must explain why your face is so pale," she said. She told him to sit up and then made him drink the water. "Does that feel better? You got some sleep now?"

"Yeah. Yeah, it does. Thanks."

"Maybe you want to come down and I can get you some grub."

Roy just sat there. He'd lost all his motivation for anything, no desire for food, or sex, or movement. Just lying back down on the sweaty bed was the only thing he wanted to do. Mesmerelda had reached the door and she stopped and turned.

"You coming?" Roy took a deep breath and lifted himself off the bed. "Atta boy. You'll feel better with some food in you. What are you in the mood for?"

"Grease," he said.

"Just my style! Ah'll make you some bacon and eggs."

They went downstairs and she began to cook.

"What time is it?" asked Roy.

"Just after seven," she said. "Almost night time."

"When do your guests arrive?"

"Not till later. You still have a few hours if you want to avoid them. Here you go, enjoy."

Roy ate like he hadn't seen food in weeks, and Mesmerelda remarked on how hungry he must have been. He finished up a second helping in record time.

"If you want you can grab a glass of whiskey from the sitting room for yourself, while ah clean up."

"Hm. I don't know. Thins the blood. I think I've been drinking a little too much lately anyway."

"Sometimes that can be a good thing."

"What the hell, eh?"

He got up and walked over to the sitting room, picked up a fresh crystal glass and put some ice and whiskey in it. Swirled the coppery liquid in the glass for a minute, listening to the tinkling of the ice.

How much older was Mesmerelda than he was? Just a curious random thought of his, as he remembered looking at her body while she cooked him his dinner.

He went back through the foyer to the kitchen and stood in the doorway with his drink. Mesmerelda was bending over as she put the frying pan away in a cupboard.

"Lovely place you got there," said Roy, and she turned and gave him a big smile as she rolled her eyes.

"You men, you're all alike," she said. Roy was in love with her bright red hair and the fact that she'd put on red lipstick to boot. "Why don't you come in and sit down?"

"I...sure..."

It just caught his attention as he pulled away from the wall. The grainy old photograph, like the J.F.K. photos of American history, but this one was much older and it was faded and looked more like it had been taken in shades of brown. Roy picked it up. He looked at the back first. It said:

Millicent Gifford, 1952

Then he turned it over.

"Oh dear Lord," he breathed to himself. He put his drink down on the side table loud enough for Mesmerelda to notice.

"Where are you going?" she said, moving to the kitchen door. Roy had slipped on his shoes in a hurry and was making his way to the door in a rush.

"Thanks for everything," Mesmerelda. "I really gotta go now. I'll send you some money for the room as soon as I can. I gotta go." He rushed out the door and down the steps of the porch and was on the dusty road back to town before he could even think of turning back.

Mesmerelda called after him, "Roy, please come back! You can stay the night here for free if you want! Just come back, it ain't safe out there!"

Roy had his back to her and just waved up his hand in a good-bye gesture, if he'd even heard her at all.

"It ain't safe out there!" she called again. But this time he was certainly out of earshot. Dusk was now upon the town of Lebanon Junction, Kentucky. She let out a deep breath and closed the door to her empty whorehouse. She stood there for one moment and put her hand to the doorframe, looking at her glossy, blood red nails, her expression reflective.

She went to the side table and picked up the grainy old picture of Millicent Gifford. And smiled.

It was her, he thought to himself as he walked hurriedly down the dusty road back to the main street. He remembered every little detail of the crinkled photograph: the sun-bleached brown pig tails, the large, effervescent smile, the cut off jeans and the plaid top tied up over the stomach.

Dear Lord it was her, and every bit of that dream I had was real, every event since I saw her must have been some sort of clash with reality. My mind meshing with madness.

Still a bit of light out. Still time to make it there. He hurried down the street and hoped and prayed he didn't run into the deputy right now. He didn't have time for a 'showdown at sunset.' He got to the bar and wasted no time; he banged on the door and yelled.

"Scooter, open the fucking door! Open up! God damn you open the door!"

No answer.

He yelled again to no avail and put his shoulder to the door to try and force it. It gave with three blows and Roy didn't waste any time in being surprised because he noticed the dead wood around the lock.

He walked in, trailing dusty motes and fading rays of pale yellow light. The interior looked blue from the dim gloom and seedy atmosphere that was prevalent in the empty establishment. Roy breathed out a small sigh in frustration.

"Scooter?" he said quietly. He didn't like the sound of his own voice in the emptiness. It was much too similar to the sound of his voice in the loneliness of the forest.

He walked in a few steps, and all the typically eerie noises affected him: the creak of the floor boards beneath his feet with every step he took, the laboured sound of his breathing, the very settling of the foundation.

"Scooter?" he called again, thinking he must be here by now. He must be opening for business by nightfall. Roy made his way towards the back to see if he was maybe in the back room.

(Then why wouldn't he have answered when called?)

He fearfully, nervously pushed open the storeroom door.
Inside was totally dark, and he could feel his heart thumping away
rapidly in his chest as he reached around for the light switch.

Dis place a hot hellhole, you hear me? Get out now.

His hand groped along the wall, hoping against hope it would
find nothing other than the light switch. Not anything slimy, nor living,
nor sharp like a six-inch knife-

He clicked on the light.

Beer! Oh dear glorious beer! Kegs and kegs and cases upon
cases alongside sixty ounce bottles of every kind of liquor imaginable.
They were all here: Coors, Budweiser, even the refreshingly familiar
Molson's from Canada. He leaned up against the door frame and tilted
his head back as though he were...well, enjoying a frosty mug of cold
beer.

Don't I feel like a fucking idiot, he said to himself. He let
himself relax a bit. *I think I'm driving myself nuts,* he thought.

He clicked off the light and turned around.

"Holy fucking Jesus!" he said, and jumped back up against the
wall startled. On the top of the bar was Scooter's hair, the dread locks

in a wicked tree-like arrangement. "That certainly wasn't there when I walked in."

He went over to the bar, slowly, looking around for any sign of another intruder who may have placed this there when he wasn't looking. But that was certainly impossible, for surely he would have heard whoever it was moving behind him. Unless maybe it was...a ghost?

There was an object under the tree hair, slick and wet and red. Roy couldn't quite make it out underneath the mass of hair. He lifted up the hair of his friend, the one who'd warned him to stay away, so he could get a better look at what it was underneath.

Go find the Black Hand.

It was Scooter's hand.

Twelve: It's Better Just to Keep your Fool Mouth Shut

"Shit hell, he's lost a lot of blood."

"Let's get him up in the truck. C'mon, we got no choice. Careful, there's lots of rust, we don't want to get all infected."

He'd heard them pull up, and the headlights of the light blue old-fashioned Ford pick-up had made him open his eyes a little. But he was too woozy to do anything about it. He felt even lighter when they picked him up.

"Ha! I bled all over my white shirt," said Roy. "Look at it. After a while it isn't red anymore. It turns...what is that? Black? Brown? Looks like I shat all over myself. Shat's a word isn't it? I had this dream

I cut my wrists and they just split right open on me and now I got shit on my white T-shirt. Must've been the knife I took to em."

"Ah got some gauze and bandage in the glove box. Keep him talking, he must be near shock by now with all of his babbling."

"Reg, you're a fucking raving alcoholic."

Reg just ignored him with utmost stoicism as he surveyed the area.

"How much time we got, Reg?"

"We're out of time, Donny-boy. Once the suns down we ain't got no time," he said, his eyes glassy and his voice a little bit contemplative.

"We should've stayed in our homes, huh, Reg?"

Reg chewed a little bit, still looking around.

"When a man lets out a stark raving scream like the one we heard, you got to get out an help him. Ain't worth being alive if you ain't gonna be a good citizen. Ah better get the gauze."

He hopped out of the flat bed and opened the door, stuck his head in and reached around in the glove box.

"Shit, Reg, he's freaking on me!" called Donny-boy. Reg rushed over and hopped back into the flat bed and they both held Roy down while he screamed and raved.

"I can feel someone watching me! Let me go you bastards! Let me out of here, I just wanna run and die! For fuck's sake let me go, I know someone's watching me! The Devil's got his eyes on me!"

Reg and Donny-boy succeeded in pinning him by holding tight to Roy's throbbing, bleeding wrists. They put enough pressure on the nerves in his arms that he held still but he screamed, at which point Reg smothered his mouth shut to quiet him.

"Now you listen to me, boy. You got to be quiet, real quiet like. Ah got some gauze and ah'm gonna patch up these wrists of yours until we can get you somewhere safe. But you got to be quiet like. No more screaming, hear?"

"I know somebody's watching me," whispered Roy, his body shuddering, his breath cold and weak. Reg and Donny-boy each took a length of gauze and one of Roy's wrists and began to wrap his wounds up tightly. "Someone won't let me leave here."

"Man, Reg, he's bleeding bad," said Donny-boy, shaking his head in hopelessness. "Ah don't think he's gonna make it."

"Now don't you go all fluffy on me, Donny, ah got one guy bleedin' to death in my truck and going all nutso. Ah can't afford to haul two of you around on my back."

"They're comin', Reg. Ah can hear em. You hear that? That's wings beating the air. They're coming."

"There ain't nothin'. It's all quiet out there. You're just being a chicken-shit. Need a night-light or something."

"Reg, man, they'll smell him. You know how they can smell blood a mile away. This guys all covered in blood an it's all over the back of the truck. They're gonna chase us down an' we can't lose them."

"Donny, I'm almost forty years old and ah lived in this town all my life and ah ain't never been caught by a vampire. Ain't much of a dumb hick as people make me out to be. Now let's get moving before ah eat my words."

Donny-boy, with no hesitation whatsoever, got up and made ready for an Olympic leap over the side of the rusty light blue pick-up, but Reg grabbed his arm and stopped him.

"Whoa, whoa, wait a minute, Donny-boy, we got to check him first. No use driving away if he's gonna turn into a vampire and smash through the back window."

"So what are you waiting for?"

"Check him, Donny."

"Aw, geez, why do ah always have to check them?"

"Just unzip his freaking pants and check him."

"Look, man, the guy tried to kill himself, Reg, he ain't no vampire, he's just nuts."

Reg took hold of Donny-boy by the green tank top he was wearing and pulled him so they were nose to nose over top of Roy's body.

"You ever see a man who's been turned into a vampire, Donny-boy? They know what's happening to them, and it drives them nuts. Ah once seen a man do worse to himself them just slit his wrists. Ah seen a man try to pull out his intestines like a magician pulling out a handkerchief. Now check him."

He let go of Donny-boy and Donny reluctantly acquiesced and unzipped Roy's pants. He pulled down the boxer shorts and muttered, "You'd be the one checking if it was a woman here. There," he said, proudly, "he's clean."

"Check the underside of it, boy, vampires ain't stupid."

"Aw, jeez hell. This thing better not move when ah touch it."

He reached down and pinched the top of it, trying to lift it by touching it as little as possible, then pulled it up.

"There. You satisfied now? Not a mark."

"Good. That wasn't so bad now was it? Let's get outta here."

They hopped in the front of the truck and Reg started her up and did a half donut, kicking up dirt and gravel as he began to drive like a lunatic for his home. They kept the back window open so they could keep an eye on Roy, and Donny-boy kept looking back at him, half scared he'd see a vampire shredding the red and white gauze wrappings around Roy's wrists. Or Roy himself, his bloody arms hanging at his sides, his eyes fierce with carmine hunger as he fixed his gaze upon Donny-boy's greasy sun-tanned neck.

"Did you hear something?"

"Shut up, Donny-boy."

"Naw, Reg, ah thought ah heard something."

Thunk.

"There, what was that? Something on the roof of the truck!"

"That's just your stupid head hitting the roof when we go over a bump."

"Oh, shit, Reg, what you going this way for?"

"Because it's the fastest way home, shithead."

"It's right by the graveyard, though."

Thunk!

"Aw, fuck, you had to hear that!"

"One grave don't make a graveyard, Donny-boy."

"It's Ray McMickle's grave man!"

Thunkthunkthunkthunkthunk!

"Aw, fuck, ah'm getting outta here!"

Reg grabbed him by the arm before he could swing open the door and throw himself out onto the dusty road whizzing by at sixty miles an hour.

"Don't be a fool, Donny-boy. You don't have a chance out there on your own."

"There's something on the roof of the truck, man! Don't tell me you don't hear that!"

"Jeez, hell, Donny-boy, we're almost there, don't be a fool!"

"Fuck fuck fuck!" yelled Donny-boy, banging his fists on the dash. He could still hear the banging on the top of the truck but Reg maintained it was only the rocks and such that were being kicked up because he was driving so fast.

They reached Reg's place, just on the outskirts of the town, well away from the dead main street so reminiscent of idyllic American life one would see in old photographs. They got out of the truck and went round the back to get Roy's half dead and blood-caked body out.

Just as Reg was bracing his thick arms on the rusty side panel to lift himself into the back he looked out across the black, lifeless panorama of the countryside. It was so black that it paradoxically had

utter depth yet no depth at all to it.

"See, Donny-boy. You and your fool head got all in a tizzy for

nothing. Now help me load this guy on my back and you go get the

door."

"Yeah. Yeah, that's right, Reg, me an my fool head. Not a thing

out there. Otherwise we'd have been toast before we'd a known it."

They picked up Roy's body and heaved it over Reg's big, sweaty

shoulder and Reg hopped off the truck and carried him to the door as

though he was weightless. Donny-boy turned to jump off the other side

of the truck and caught a glimpse of the dent marks that dotted the roof

of the pick-up like machine gun fire. But this time he kept his fool

mouth shut.

He didn't think he would open his eyes to sunlight again. It

didn't carry with it the sense of relief that one would think it would,

especially for a man in his situation: sunlight blinding his vision meant it

was daylight and he was alive. Most would be flooded with a pervading sense of quiet satisfaction and thankfulness but Roy only felt frustrated and depressed. He had the sense of a man who was certainly doomed.

But once again he picked his head up off the bed, and he didn't really care that the sheets looked like they used to be white.

"You're up."

"In a sense of the word."

"Reg is out back chopping wood. Gonna get the outdoor grill going and make us some food."

"What's for breakfast? Wait, don't tell me. Possum."

Donny-boy was chewing some tobacco and he broke into a wide, brown-toothed grin.

"Nothing wrong with a little possum, city-boy."

Roy rubbed and stretched his neck and cracked his joints to relieve the stiffness. He noticed the red/black/white bandages around his wrists.

"What am I doing here?" he asked.

"You was screaming out on the street last night. Me and Reg heard you on our way home. You tried to kill yourself last night."

Roy picked up his arms and looked closely at the bloody bandages.

"Doesn't sound like something I'd do," he said. But his voice didn't carry with it the conviction of a man who was absolutely certain of himself.

"Way ah reckon," said Donny-boy, getting up off his stool and pushing his ample stomach outwards, "Man doesn't usually picture his own death. Less he's real down or something. You down on your luck, mister?"

"Guess you could say that. I picked up and left everything I'd ever known and now I'm nowhere. Middle of fucking nowhere. And I'm stuck here."

He got up and went over to the window and looked outside, his expression reflective. He tried to remember everything that had happened to him since he'd left Winnipeg but he couldn't make some sense or order of the events. Not that he really wanted to. He heard an axe falling and craned his neck and saw Reg chopping the wood.

And in the far, far distance he saw one lone grave. It stood out because it was a slick, stone grey, very dark, like clouds before a thunderstorm. The muted grey colour stood out, bold against the sandy grey of the dirt road. The wind picked up and blew enough dirt around to hide the grave from view, and Roy remarked to himself at how angry the wind seemed, how <u>human</u>.

"Why are you here?" he asked.

"Me and Reg, we were born here. This is our home."

Roy turned away from the window and looked at him.

"But there's nothing here," he said. "I don't see any people, I don't see any cars around. Nothing. It's like this town's dead."

"Then why are you here, stranger?"

"Because it won't let me leave. Man, I just wanna walk out the door and down the road till I find the next town but I'm scared to hell that I'm just gonna come back in the other side. I can't even sleep at night anymore. I don't know why but I keep having these awful dreams."

"Maybe a dead town's giving you nightmares too."

"If this town's dead then why are you guys still here?"

"Nothing's completely dead, stranger. Everywhere's got its survivors."

"So why are all the rest of the people dead?"

"Don't know how to survive, ah guess."

"What are they surviving from!" yelled Roy, banging his fist on a wooden crate that was a bedside table. Donny-boy just sat there as calm as a deer at a lake, chewing his tobacco. Reg walked in from outside with his axe hanging in his hand.

"What the hell's going on here?" he said. "Boy, you better calm down and relax if you wanna stay a guest in my house. Food's gonna be cooking shortly." He put his axe over his shoulder and walked back outside.

It was quiet for a moment and Roy lowered his head and half buried it in a hand. He listened to the spit and tobacco swishing around in Donny-boy's mouth for a moment just to distract himself from thinking of anything else.

"This town's haunted isn't it," said Roy.

"Wouldn't know," said Donny-boy, chewing. "Ah never been to any other town."

"Shit, do I ever want to get out of here," he said, looking upwards as though speaking to God when in reality he was only speaking to Donny-boy.

"Then why don't you just leave?" said Donny-boy.

"Don't you understand, I can't!" he said, raising his voice again and gesturing with his hand as though he were spitting the words out. He let out a breath in frustration. But what would happen if he were to continue on down the road leading away from Reg's little shack of a place? Was he caught in some cosmic black hole on earth that sucked up lost and wandering souls?

Reg called from outside: "Grub's on!" And they went out and sat on a log around a fire and a steel grill with pots and pans on it. The food was ready shortly; ham-steaks, beans, bacon and corn and they sat around the fire in the late afternoon sun eating.

"So what's down the road there?" asked Roy, actually enjoying the food. He tried to eat slow and enjoy it but the wind picked up every so often and blew the dirt around and some of it got in his food.

"Not really sure," said Reg, smacking his lips with the barbecue sauce. "Forest I reckon."

Hm, forest, thought Roy. And I'm sure if I go down there I'll just end up getting lost and get spit back into town.

"You guys never been down there?"

"Never had to," said Donny-boy. "Got everything we need right here."

"Wait a minute," said Roy, putting down his corn. "You mean to tell me you two have really never left this town."

"Never had a reason to," said Donny-boy.

"We were born here, we live here, and we're gonna die here," said Reg. "You big city folk live life so fast you forgot small town values. We don't go in for no moving here and there shenanigans."

"Scooter's dead," said Roy, his voice deadpan.

"Ah say's pardon?" said Reg.

"Scooter," reiterated Roy. "The guy who ran the tavern. He's dead."

"Who's Scooter?" asked Donny-boy.

"Remember when we met in the local bar on Main street? The bartender?"

Roy looked back and forth between the two of them and it was obvious they didn't know whom he was talking about. More obvious they were more interested in gobbling up the ham hanging from their mouths. Had they forgotten? Was Scooter forever wiped from their memories by the evil influence of Ray McMickle?

"You guys have no idea who I'm talking about."

"Haven't a clue."

They went back to their food, and there was a lull in the conversation, mostly because Reg and Donny-boy were ravenously hungry and Roy was stunned into silence by the pair's 'amnesia.'

"Who's grave is that over there," said Roy, and he gestured down the road.

"C'mon, boy you'd better eat up, ah wanna put this fire out before dark."

"We've got hours. Who's grave is that."

Neither of them said anything.

"Why do you have to have the fire out before dark."

Nary a word from either of them.

"Reg, you're a fucking asshole. Answer my questions."

Reg stood up in his dirty tank top, fat beer gut protruding from underneath. He turned around and put his plate down on the log, and if Roy hadn't been so angry he would have winced at the builder's cleavage.

Reg turned back around and he met Roy's unwavering gaze.

"Boy, you show some respect to me in my home. Ah hauled your ass out of the dead of night and put you up and fed you. Ah don't deserve that kind of a talking to."

Roy's mouth hardened and he still tried to pierce Reg with his gaze but he could see that Reg wouldn't back down. As uncultured as he may have seemed, this was a moral issue for him; and he was a strongly moral man who stood by his convictions. And Roy figured he would get the shit kicked out of him if he didn't soften his stand, so he eased up. But Reg was still standing there, though he seemed a little less defensive. Perhaps he was just waiting for an apology?

"Wait," said Roy. "The ham. It came in a package. Where did you get it from?"

"Boy are you dense?" said Reg. "Got it from the store, where else?"

"And who runs the store?" asked Roy.

"What do you mean?" asked Reg.

"When you went to the store, how did you get the meat?"

"Just walked into the store an took what we needed and left."

"So you just stole it?"

"You calling me a thief, boy?" said Reg, hands on hips.

"No, no," said Roy, trying to ease off any confrontation. "Does the store ever run out of meat?"

"Hm," thought Reg. "None that ah can ever remember. Donny?"

Donny shook his head.

"So what would you do if the store ran out of meat?" asked Roy.

"Figure if we had a problem we'd just tell Deputy Kuthrow."

"Deputy Kuthrow..." said Roy, quietly and more to himself. "Who's grave is that down the road?"

Reg took his hands off his hips and gave his belly a bit of a scratch. He adjusted his jeans and sat down on the log and looked over at Donny-boy, who just lit up a cigarette and said nothing.

"That's a part of our history we ain't very proud of," said Reg. "The grave belongs to Ray McMickle. He was a notorious serial killer back in the day. This here was a nice, peaceful town, everything anyone who wanted to get away could hope for. Then Ray McMickle went on a killing spree just before he graduated high school. How old was he Donny-boy?"

"Reckon eighteen or so if he was graduating high school," said Donny-boy with a shrug.

"Yeah, eighteen. Boy had all he could have going for him. Anyways, story goes he just up and disappears and all of a sudden like people start turning up murdered. Brutally. Strung up on trees and when they take them down they find that they been slit all the way up to the back of their neck and an ice-pick wedged in there.

"Or there was one that was hanging by a branch by their leg and the other was twenty feet away and the only reason the Sheriff found it was because their entrails made a path to it.

"And the one they dredged up out of the lake in the middle of the woods. You remember that one Donny-boy?"

Donny nodded grimly as he sat there with his knees up and a cigarette smoking away in his hand. Roy wondered why he felt like it was night as they sat around the fire even though it was just mid-afternoon.

"Yeah. Dredged one out of the lake and she was all blue like ice and her throat ripped out like someone had exploded it open with dynamite. God rest their souls," he said, and he kissed the tiny gold crucifix that hung at his neck.

"They say that Ray got mixed up in some kind of Satanism or black magic or something," said Donny-boy. "He was supposed to take that sweet Milly Gifford girl to the prom but she was all stood up and ended up going on her own. Never showed up there and people started to talk a bit because of all the killing but figured she was just taking her time all broken up on account a losing her boyfriend. She showed up all right. Ray had caught her and did a number on her too and brought her body to the school parking lot and...What was that word again, Reg?"

"Necromania."

"Yeah. That was it. Necromania. Kind of a cool sounding word if you forget what it is."

"So where'd they bury Milly?"

"Cemetery. They put Ray's body here because no one wanted him buried near their loved ones," said Donny.

"Wait a minute. Ray killed Milly, but how did Ray die?"

"Just a sec," said Donny. "Ah think we got some newspaper clipping's in a scrapbook." He went into the house and came out a short moment later. "Yeah. Yeah, here it is. Ray McMickle, shot dead. Closed casket funeral."

"Just shot him?" said Roy, a little surprised.

"Uh huh," said Donny-boy, holding the scrapbook like he was reading a newspaper. "Caught him running from the high school and the Sheriff at the time was out patrolling around, especially near the school because of the prom. Heard the commotion and spotted him and shot him once in the back with a shotgun, then the head and that was it. Buried the next day right over there." He gestured with his chin towards the grave just down the road.

"And everyone saw him buried," said Roy. The two men nodded. "Well what about his family? His house? Milly?"

"Family abandoned the house the next day," said Reg. "Just picked up and moved on, never heard from again. Boarded up the windows and no one ever went there. Kids never even went in there to tell ghost stories or nothing. Too much respect...or maybe too much fear. Milly ah don't know. What happened to Milly, Donny?"

"Reckon they just buried her. Family was never the same after that. Can't say ah blame them either."

"So where are the Giffords now?" said Roy, digging.

"Left as fast as the McMickles did. Situation like that tore the whole town clean apart. Been dead or dying ever since."

(Roy.)

"Jesus, who the fuck said that?" screamed Roy. Reg and Donny both stiffened, bewildered, as Roy leapt up from his seat and knocked over the remains of his meal. He shook and looked chilly, as though someone had dropped ice down the spine of his shirt. He grabbed his head.

"Shit, sorry guys, I'm really sorry. Man I could've sworn someone said my name, a girl. Fuck. I'm going nuts." Roy sat down and shivered despite the intense heat. "Sorry. For the past two days I've hardly slept and I've been listening to ghost stories and tales of serial killers. I'm just really peaked out." Roy hugged his arms around himself and said, against his own better judgment, "You have a picture of this McMickle guy?"

"Reckon ah do," said Donny, and flipped through the pages of the scrapbook. "Yep. Here you go." He handed Roy the scrapbook.

"He doesn't look so All-American," said Roy. The man in the picture had a five o'clock shadow on his face and hard, hollow, blue eyes, and his hair looked greasy and black and was combed from one side of his head to the other. "I thought you said they shot him right away, no trial, no nothing."

"Yep," said Donny-boy.

"Then how'd they get this picture?"

"They took that one after he was dead."

"Fucking Christ," said Roy, but his eyes were still fixed upon the grainy brown image on the newsprint. After a moment he flipped through the pages of the scrapbook, looking at the headlines of the articles. "Hm," he mused.

"Find, something, stranger?" said Reg.

"Says here that they never found Milly's body. 'Ray McMickle was seen fornicating with the body of Millicent Gifford in the parking lot of Wayford County High School. One student approached the suspect and was stabbed by McMickle before he could take any action, but he did notice with utmost certainty that Millicent Gifford was not responding to him in any way whatsoever. McMickle then proceeded to attempt a getaway in a vehicle. He was found only minutes later by the Wayford County Sheriff running away from his vehicle and was taken down in one attempt by shotgun and pronounced dead on the scene. A week long search for the body of Millicent Gifford ended in failure.'"

(ROY!)

He most certainly heard that voice, but he jumped because he felt something touch his shoulder. It was Millicent Gifford.

Thirteen: Memories of the Old Haunted House

And she was standing in front of Ray McMickle's house. She bit her lower lip and twisted slowly from side to side. Small town and sexy and oh so come hither.

"Ah was hoping you'd come back," she said to him as he stood at the end of the walkway to the porch.

"Well, I thought that that was Mesmerelda's slogan for this place. Keep 'em comin."

The sun was just setting down on the horizon, making a grapefruit mirage of it. Reg and Donny-boy wouldn't come near the house. They denied it was haunted, they denied the existence of anything beyond the borders of Lebanon Junction, Kentucky, but they wouldn't come near the house.

"Why the hell not?" asked Roy, flabbergasted.

Reg had leaned in close to him and said, in hushed tones as though the people who weren't around would hear, "Vampires. Blood-sucking demons. You wonder..." he said, pointing a finger at Roy, "You wonder why you been having nightmares since you got here. You wonder why you can't leave. It ain't ghosts. You call me a slack-jawed, dim-witted yokel but it ain't ghosts man. It's vampires. Plain and simple. And they haunt you."

"Then why don't you leave, Reg?" *You fat, greasy bastard,* thought Roy.

"Ah was born in Lebanon Junction and ah'll die in Lebanon Junction," he said. "But ah'm a survivor. Ain't no vampire gonna kill me. And ah ain't stupid enough to be out in the middle of the night with vampires roaming around." And he and Donny-boy drove off.

Fuckin' hell, thought Roy. *Call me a stupid city boy. This is all a figment of my imagination. Yes. That's it. I am going nuts. There are no vampires here. There can't be. There are no people to feed on. I am here by myself. Reg and Donny-boy are Jerry Springer rejects from the lowest common denominator of my brain. There is nobody here but me. This is a ghost town. The only thing here is ghosts.*

Ghosts...Milly.

"Ah'm so glad you came back," she said, and she was close to him now. "Ah thought ah may have scared you off. Ah tend to do that to people sometimes."

"You aren't real, Milly." He closed his eyes for a second. "Just my imagination. This is a ghost town. Just a ghost. I can only see you because I'm here. Then why are you solid?"

"Don't you remember feeling me, Ray? How good it felt? Ah just wanted to make you happy. Ah just wanted to keep you here."

"No. You aren't real. I'm just nuts."

The worst thing...is when they touch you.

"Oh, God, Milly, I can feel you."

She had her arms around him and he tried to hesitate but he found himself wrapping his arms around her as well.

Why does she feel so real? he thought. But how is a ghost supposed to feel? Like a memory, perhaps. But whose memory was he experiencing? And why?

"Ah love it when ah'm in your arms, Ray. Ah don't ever want to let you go."

"Ah don't want to let you go either, Milly."

"Tell me why again, Ray."

"Because ah love you."

He felt such a swoon, as though a breeze had picked up and rocked them back and forth in its arms. It was afternoon again, late afternoon, and the air was dewy as much as Milly's eyes were.

"Make love to me, Ray. Ah want you to."

"Prom's only three months away."

"Ah don't care, Ray. It'll still be special. Please? Your house is empty now, too."

For one moment all existence melted in anticipation as their lips met, and neither of them had realized that they'd even tilted their heads to kiss. And the swoon returned as their tongues danced in each other's mouths, as they forgot about school and the rest of their lives that they had ahead of them because the only thing they knew was this one brief and luxurious moment. And they were swept up in it, and swept up to the bedroom and in moments found themselves lying next to each other naked in the sweet, wet Kentucky heat of late afternoon.

For several minutes they lay next to each other, doing nothing but basking, and they were like babies lying there, just born and naked.

"It's so beautiful," Ray, she said, looking down at him. "Ah just love him. You think he loves me?"

"Oh, he certainly does, darlin'."

"Then why ain't he movin'?" she said, flashing a toothy grin and girlish giggle.

"Ah must admit, Millicent," he said, soberly, "ah am a bit nervous."

"Ray," she said, matching his solemnity, "ah am too." Then she burst out into a bubbly laugh. "The two people voted most likely to succeed and were both having the jitters before making love!"

All it required was the deft sword of seduction:

"What are you gonna do for me, Milly?"

"Anything you want," she said, and she was stern and serious again and she held his stare as she gave him her answer. Then she half sat up and moved closer to his hips and put her lips gently on them.

"Ah'm sure you'll love this," she said in a whisper. Then, "Ray," and a smile as she looked up for a second, "ah think it moved."

He smiled back but didn't answer.

"What if ah put my mouth so close you can feel my breath on it."

"Yeah."

"Can you feel my breath on it?"

"Yeah."

"Ah think it moved."

"Yeah."

"Do you want me to put my lips on it?"

"Oh yeah."

"Just my lips, or my whole mouth?"

"Are you teasing me?"

"Maybe a little."

"Are you nervous?"

"About what?"

"Putting your lips on it."

"Somewhat. Ah just want to make you happy."

"You do. Very happy."

"Ah just want you to like it."

"Ah will. Ah guarantee ah will."

"Promise?"

"Promise."

She took the plunge. She lifted it gently between her thumb and forefinger and pointed it at her mouth and then pressed the pink, wet membrane of her cheeks and her tongue firmly around it. She slid from the base to the head as she felt him harden inside her.

"Mmm, you taste so good," she said. She took him again and watched as his body stiffened and shuddered in pleasure. "Where do you feel it, Ray? Do you just feel it here or do you feel it all over?"

"All over," he said, his voice barely above a whisper, and breathy as his head lolled onto its side.

"Do you want to touch my breasts?" she said.

"Yeah."

"Do you want me to stop?"

"No," he said.

"You have to choose. Ah can't keep going if you want to touch my breasts."

She got up and stood on her knees on the bed and pushed her chest out a bit to tantalize him. He looked up from his prone position and smiled at her.

"Touch my breasts, Ray. You know you want to."

He sat up a little bit and put one hand on her back to support her and with his other hand he cupped her full breast and fondled it, pushing it up and around and squeezing it gently.

"Oh ah love it," she said. "Your hands are so warm." He let go and he fondled her nipple with his finger, pushing it inwards and then making circles around the edge of it. "Oh, God, yeah, that feels so good, squeeze it again." And she grabbed her other breast so she could feel warmth in both of them.

He pushed her down by her chest onto the bed and as her leg slid out from underneath her body they became entangled with his. She tried to smile but a great warmth of solemnity washed over them and it felt inappropriate for her to do so even though she was happier at this moment than she could ever remember herself being.

She was lying on the bed now, her body before his, and he was still ready for her. Her knees were bent, pointed inwards a bit, and he had to push them apart to open her up. But she let him, even though she shook with vulnerability and felt the slightest shudder of cold up her spine like a winter draft from an open window. He lowered his head to her hips, closed his eyes, and inhaled.

"Can you smell me?" she asked him.

"Yeah," he said.

"Do you like it?"

"Oh yeah," he said. "Definitely."

"Touch me there, Ray. With your fingers." He gently breached her lips. "What does it feel like?"

"Your mouth," he said.

"But better? Softer?"

"Yeah. Better."

"Can you make love to me now? Can you pretend it's the prom?"

"I'm dying to, Milly," he said, and moved up and pressed his chest to hers. His lips met with hers and his hips with hers as well and he pressed himself into her and for just a second he thought he'd hurt her when she said, "Oh!" but it was simply for pleasure.

"This is all of it, Ray. That swoon ah felt out there, it ain't nothing compared to this. This is everything. This is it."

And they made love for nearly an hour and their skin became dewy wet like the Kentucky air as their passions swelled.

"Ray," she said, her eyes all glassy and misty as she felt him moving within her, her body not her own anymore. "Ray," she said again, trying to distract him from the task that she didn't want him to be distracted from.

"Yeah," he said, stopping for a moment, his voice betraying the fact that the magic had been lost with the interruption.

"Can you save yourself for me?"

"What do you mean?"

"Can you just stop making love to me an then we can save the end for the prom? It'll be like waiting."

"Ah don't know if ah can, Milly."

"Please? It'll be so beautiful. Just waiting for that night to come an knowing were gonna finish what we started here."

He knelt between her legs, his face expressionless, his body motionless, the tip of him still inside of her. Milly wasn't sure what to think, as she lay before him naked, holding him between her legs. Had she disappointed him? Had she angered him and he was just afraid to show it? Or had she done both.

But then he smiled.

And she smiled back at him too. She softened and let her hands fall off her chest and her breasts quivered just a bit with her movement. She took his hands and she felt as though the separateness of their souls had been diminished as thin as it could ever be between two people. So she matched his smile whenever he smiled at her, just to know that they were bonded in some way, in happiness. She moved his hands downwards, towards her hips, so she could feel their large, strong presence there, and the whole time they held each other's gaze. She moved his hands closer together. He felt a bit of soft, light blond hair touch his hands. He looked down at her.

And his smile faded.

"Whore," he said.

"What?" she said, utterly startled by his unexpected reaction.

"You didn't bleed," he said. "You're a whore." He might as well have stabbed her in the neck with a knife rather than use that word.

"Oh God, Ray, please, ah thought you knew," she cried.

"How many," he said, his voice terse and vengeful.

"Ray, ah don't like the look in your eyes," she said.

"How...fucking...many..."

"Please, Ray," she said, crying now, completely crying. She sat up and leaned forward and tried to take hold of his thing to satisfy him, to placate him. He picked her up by the arms and flung her against the headboard of the great bed where they shared their love moments ago. It broke the plaster of the wall behind it and Milly broke into a torrent of tears, feeling her back turn red in anticipation of tomorrow's bruises.

"How fucking many," said Ray again.

"Oh, fuck, don't make me say it," she said, doubling over as her soul was in utter agony, her words dripping with tears. "Please don't make me say it. Don't make me hate you, don't make me hurt you."

He had her by the neck now, holding her up against the wall. She didn't see his clenched fist rearing back behind his head because her eyes were filled with tears and her neck was being painfully constricted by his hands, his fingers digging into her skin, and the pain itself blinded her. But she could sense her life at risk because she felt the heat of his anger through his fingers.

"Please God, ah'll tell, please, just put me down, ah can't breathe anymore," she said, and he let her drop with a bounce back onto the mattress. She doubled over again and choked and coughed to get the air back into her lungs and if she'd had any sense of serenity she would have thought how appropriate it was that she was naked while her life was being threatened. "Twenty-seven," she said, crying on the words, her breath choked and staccato. "You fuckin' happy now? Ah've slept with twenty-seven men."

Ray looked at her for a moment and then got up off the bed and went over to the window and stood there naked, looking out of it. Milly was still on the bed, doubled over to hide her nakedness, to hide her face that was flushed wet hot with water. She was, plainly and simply, scared. Scared because she was naked and hurt, scared because of how tranquil Ray was as he stood looking out the window.

"Ah'll do anything," she whispered through her tears. "Please, Ray, ah'll do anything. Just love me again. Ah need you."

He turned his head slowly away from the window. It was so scary how calm he was. She wished he were angry again. She wished he were hitting her again. At least that would be normal. At least that would be expected. Now she was scared in her mind and that was much worse than being scared for her body.

He moved over to her and grabbed her wrists and pulled her up roughly so her face was threateningly close to his deep red eyes.

"Would you bleed for me, Milly?" he said, and his lip sneered sinisterly when he said bleed.

"Ah'd do anything to make you mine again, Ray," she said, and truly meant it, perhaps because of the intense, quiet fear she felt washing over her body.

"Would you bleed for me, Milly," he said again. She slowly, timidly, nodded her head yes. A small smile finally broke on his lips and he pulled her off the bed by her wrists and dragged her to the hallway, her legs struggling to keep up with him.

"You're no better than the whores that come in and out of this house," he said, and she was a little bit relieved because he seemed angry again. Maybe he would just drag her outside and beat her until she bled all over the grass. That wouldn't be so bad. Her dad had whipped her mama much worse with the metal buckle on his leather belt so she had red lashes on her cheeks and one time she nearly lost an eye. So it wouldn't be that bad if Ray just beat her till she bled on the grass enough to be forgiven for fucking too many men and then her wounds could heal and they could live happily ever after again.

But he didn't drag her outside. He took her down the stairs and, his hands gripping her wrists like shackles, her eyes looking longingly to the front door in anticipation of a final beating, he took her in a different direction and opened the door to the basement.

"R-ray, where are you taking me? It's all b-black down there."

He shoved her up against the wall and she slammed the back of her skull and she had already cried too much and been hurt too much to cry anymore. Then he dragged her again and took her down the steps and plunged the both of them into darkness.

147

She couldn't move her legs fast enough to keep up with him and she fell while being dragged and banged her knees on the stairs. She finally found the floor and they were still for a moment, and she felt something not unlike powder beneath her feet.

Her heart beat with anticipation not unlike that of the anticipation one feels when one is about to have sex and the sweat beneath her arms and along her forehead was cold.

They were completely still for a moment. He took a hand off of her wrist.

Then something hard hit her head and her eyes closed and everything was twice as black.

Something still gripped her wrists. And her ankles too. How could he have four hands? No. It wasn't his hands. It was rope. Plain and simple rope. She tried to move but she couldn't. Her arms and legs had been splayed out as far as they could possibly go and the rope was tied so tight it cut off the circulation in her extremities and turned her hands and feet white.

"Ray?" she ventured quietly. But her voice was so loud in the silence. The only sound she heard was her own breathing, and the occasional drip of water. "Ray? Ah...ah'm really scared now. Ah learned my lesson. Ah'll never have another man except you. Ah promise."

No answer. Just a drip of water.

And scared she was. More scared than she'd ever been in her life. Her legs were held firmly apart and she felt such fear and vulnerability because her vagina was exposed to the cold touch of the hand of the open air and with every little draft she tensed in fear from imagined atrocities. If Ray McMickle had sprung from the dark and pounded her with his cock or punched her in the cunt with his fist she would have screamed and thrashed no matter how hopeless it was.

"Ah saw the Black Hand," he said from the darkness. There was a bit of an echo. She couldn't place where the voice came from.

"Ray, ah'm scared, please," she pleaded. There was a faint flicker of hope because he'd spoken. She knew for certain he was still here and hadn't left her to die. (Or had he stayed to accompany her to death?)

The sound of something scraping. Then a burst of flame. He lit a white candle and it took a moment for her eyes to adjust to the light but now she could see at least. He wore a black robe, his head hooded and hidden in shadow. She hated the look in his eyes now because they were merely black pits of shadow. He held the candle before his chest in his bare hands and didn't flinch when the hot wax dripped on his fingers.

"What are you going to do to me, Ray?" she asked, her voice timorous. She knew she would regret even asking such a silly question and knew even more so and instantly when she looked around her and caught a glimpse of her surroundings in the bare light of the candle. "Oh, God, what is this?" she cried. She was at the five points. The powder she'd felt beneath her feet was the outline of the pentacle which she was now bound within, and the foreboding, hooded figure of Ray McMickle loomed over her.

"Ah'm gonna bleed you, Milly," he said. "Make you pure again."

"Oh God no, please don't, Ray. Nothing can change the past, please, ah love you now!"

He moved closer to her and extended his hands so the flame of the candle was near to her vagina.

"Oh fuck, Ray, please, don't, no, God, no don't burn me, Ray!" she screamed, but he was so obsessively focused with her private lips that he couldn't be roused from his fugue. No matter how much she screamed she couldn't get through to him. It was as though her voice wasn't being heard in this dimension.

She felt the heat of the flame of the white candle come treacherously close to her sex and she began to thrash her hips wildly as though she were fucking. Ray pulled the candle away, a little bit suddenly, as though she may have roused him somehow. He stood up from his kneeling position and backed away and Milly calmed a bit and stopped her thrashing. She picked her head up and saw Ray's black-robed back moving away from her. He reached his arm out and pulled at something on the wall. Her limbs were abruptly stretched to the point where her ligaments nearly tore, and she couldn't move at all, partly because of the pain.

"Ow, oh fuck, Ray, let me go, please!"

He turned and walked back to her and resumed his kneeling position between her legs. He put the candle so close to her that her hairs shriveled from the heat and nearly caught fire.

"Refresh the seal," he said, and his voice seemed to lose a bit of that southern drawl, as though it were not him that was speaking. He tilted the candle and let the hot wax drip from the wax cup within which the flame flickered. Milly screamed each time that the wax hit her skin, leaning her head back and wincing her eyes tight shut. He thickly coated her entire genital area with the white candle wax, and the only thing Milly was thankful for was that the wax cooled quickly and eventually protected her from Ray's further workings.

It felt like her cunt couldn't breathe.

She let out an utterly relieved breath and cleared saliva from her throat. Her chest heaved up and down as her heart thumped loudly behind her breasts and her lungs laboured for some clean air.

"That wasn't so bad, Ray," she said. "You scared me enough, now. You hurt me enough. You asked me if ah'd do anything and ah obviously would, now please let me go, Ray? Please?"

"Awaken the Beast," said Ray. Milly began to hear muttering, as though the walls had begun to chant. The words sounded like Latin or some sort of backwards ancient language.

His chest began to heave greatly beneath his robes and he raised his arms up, the black folds of robe hanging down and revealing his wrists and hands. It popped out from a part in the robes, like an actor slipping out between curtains for his accolades. His erection was stark white against the black material.

"He is awake. He asks for you. Will you have him?"

"Ah can't. You've closed me up."

He moved forward and stood over her, his legs on either side of her body, the robes draped over her and making her sick. His penis was pointing at her face now.

"Will you have him?" he reiterated.

"Y-yes," she stuttered. "If that's what it takes." She'd given a hundred blow-jobs and never before been so scared as to feel she would choke on his penis.

He moved it closer to her mouth and she sealed her lips closed in a vain show of resistance. But he was too quick for her and had exerted too much control over her by this point that the second it touched her lips she opened and it slid in until it touched the back of her throat.

At first he moved on his own, slowly going in and out of her. She was almost thankful because of his gentleness. This was a much more tranquil form of violation and she merely shivered as though cold.

Then he put his fingers near to her ears, but he didn't touch them; oh no, not touching them, as though touching her would be some sort of sacrilege at this point. He caressed the air around her ears as though they were delicate flowers just blossoming. And now her head was moving back and forth along his shaft, even though she made no effort of her own to move it. His hands had reached into some sort of internal energy, pulling at the strings of her soul to make her head move and suck him. He had truly penetrated her by this point.

"Kiss the God," she heard him whisper, his breath shuddering with pleasure. She wasn't sure if he was himself anymore, or if something had possessed his body. He certainly didn't sound like himself, and the Ray she knew could never dream of inflicting such pain upon anyone.

Her face was drying of the tears a bit. She tried to enjoy the taste of him in her mouth without thinking too much on her situation. Had his jealousy merely thrown him into a state of utter dementia? Was instilling a sexual fear in her his way of absolving himself of the thought of her sinful deeds of the past?

He began to move with her now. She felt a frenzy building but he never seemed to achieve any crescendo, nor did he throb with any climax.

She felt his hip muscles flex and the base of his penis was pushed into her lower lip. Their movements became very small and terse and his breathing matched that pace as well.

"Will you take him unto yourself," he asked, his voice booming in the cold, dank blackness of the basement. Milly tried to answer but Ray wouldn't get out of her mouth, and every time she tried to pull her mouth away he spread his fingers next to her ears again and she couldn't move her head away. "Will you take him unto yourself," and all she could do was nod her head a little bit to say yes.

He leaned his head back a little bit, pleasure washing over him as he resumed his quick little movements. He clenched his hands into fists and his arms reverberated with his spasms and Milly felt his thing throb in her mouth and his thick, viscous come splash against the back of her throat. He emptied himself in her mouth almost as though her were pissing and then pulled himself out, leaving a little bit of a mess on her lips too.

In some sick way she was enjoying this. Just because he'd stopped hurting her and it was sex she was trying to enjoy it. Sex by candlelight with white wax on her cunt and a black-robed demon in Gothic splendour. And he'd released himself into her, gave her the greatest gift as written by nature, and who knew what was carried upon the seed she just swallowed?

Ray retreated from her and knelt between her legs again. He spent a solemn moment in silence as though in prayer, and then he touched his left hand to his forehead, then to his stomach, then across from rib to rib in the symbol of an inverted cross. He pulled his hands close to his robe and gripped something.

"Bleed the Host," he said, and in his hands glinted the silver of a knife, the blade pointed to the floor. Milly's eyes went wide with horror but when she tried to scream she found that her throat had been clogged up with Ray's semen and she couldn't utter a word. Nor could she thrash because of the ropes and the pain in her ligaments. She saw him smile from behind his hood of shadows and he put a finger to his lips and said 'sh'. But he'd cruelly robbed her of the power of speech and she hoped that she hadn't said her last words in this world.

And she had some realization as to what he'd done to her. Through sex and magic he'd bound her to silence for this atrocity, and she knew he had complete control over her body and soul.

He took the knife and, like a magician performing his deadliest act, placed the tip of it to the lump of wax between her legs. Every inch of Milly's body screamed in urgency of pain but she was bound, helpless to resist. Not when she felt the hardened wax crack nor when she felt the cold steel of the blade make contact with her labia could she hope to escape.

What scared her most was the care with which Ray McMickle executed his ceremony, as though he were trying not to ruin her corpse. And if she thought she had no control over her destiny before she reached a new level of utter hopelessness; he'd inserted a blade into her and he clenched the handle to ensure that any of the slightest of movements from Milly would surely mean pain and suffering.

"Bleed the Host," he said again, his voice quieter, more reflective as if remembering the past thousand years of his demon life with sadness. He handled the knife in much the same way as he'd handled himself within her mouth, putting a firm and gentle pressure with the blade on her lower labia. And for some reason it was like pleasure when she felt her skin split and the cold of the blade was replaced with the warmth of her own blood. Perhaps because she was at this point numb that she didn't feel any overwhelming urge to scream and cry and thrash. She pictured her brilliant red blood oozing over the cracked, dirty white of the candle wax.

Milly stiffened for a moment as she felt the knife probing around within her, then she relaxed because Ray had begun to slide it out. He stuck out his tongue and wiped her blood off the knife carefully so as not to cut himself. She heard the metal chink on the floor as he put the knife down. Then he began to pick away at the wax with his fingers, and mercifully he didn't rip the whole thing off, as it would have torn out every hair that was stuck to it. But this was the scary part: the serenity of his violence, the gentle and caring touch his fingers had when they'd tortured her. For this was a man who killed what he coveted.

Most of the shell had been cleared away from the orifice to her womb. He pulled back his hood and bent his head towards her vagina and began to lick away at her cut cunt, lapping up the seeping blood much like a kitten cleans the dirt off itself. He even massaged her thighs a little bit and she hated him because she loved it.

He owned her.

She was his Satanic virgin.

And it awakened a hunger within Ray McMickle, which was never to be satiated by any earthly feast.

Oh God, Milly, I can feel it, he thought. And he wondered if she could hear his thoughts. And why shouldn't she? She was a ghost wasn't she? This was her world, wasn't it? Did Lebanon Junction, Kentucky even exist? Did the few people left within it even exist?

I can feel it.

Not her, <u>it</u>. All around him. What was it?

"It is the Black Hand."

Oh my God he heard that! Someone's voice! An actual voice! Deep...guttural...just a little guttural. Like someone who drank whiskey for a hundred years.

"What is the Black Hand?" he said. So bold he was! This veritable stranger who stood in such darkness it may have been death for all he knew. Yet he dared to ask a question.

"Can't you feel it?" said the voice. Strange to hear the tone get a little higher to emphasize the question. "Lift your arms."

"Why."

"Lift them."

Roy did so.

"It's almost like trying to push through water."

"I don't feel anything."

There was a noise like smoke seeping out from nostrils. The creature was thinking.

"Then how did you get here," said the voice.

"Who are you? Where am I?" asked Roy. Again the seeping smoke sound. Then a snapping of fingers and single white candle flickered to life.

"Oh dear God," breathed Roy. He was in the basement, standing on the white pentacle made of powder. Ahead of him he could see a man sitting upon some sort of throne and garbed in all black robes. At first Roy thought he was hooded but after a moment his eyes adjusted to the light and he tried to make out what he could among the shadows that the man had recessed himself in. The thick hair and goatee was long and scraggly and coloured black with hints of dark, dirty green. What little light from the candle there was lit up the man's skin in a ghastly, wrinkled and chalky white. The only thing that stood out about the man was that he had dim yellow eyes. "Are you Ray McMickle?"

The creature smiled a wicked and sinful smile.

"Part of me is," he said. "The body is. That's how I stay here. In this body."

"So he wasn't really a notorious serial killer. It was you."

"It was within him. He saw the Black Hand."

"What is the Black Hand?"

"Who brought you here?"

"Nobody brought me here."

"You cannot see the Hand. Someone brought you here."

"How come I'm not tied up," said Roy, his voice flat. The creature smiled once again.

"Who ever said you were free?"

"Is this the whore house?" asked Roy, looking up at the ceiling.

"Whore's come here, yes. One even lay upon the spot you stand now."

"How come I'm not dead yet?"

"Who ever said you are not?"

The creature got up, seemingly blasé about attending to Roy at all. He slowly swaggered along the edge of the wall, some of the light from the candle following him.

"I sealed her up and broke her again in the name of Satan. I supped on her blood."

"Is that how you live? On blood?"

"Who brought you here?" he said, his eyes blazing yellow and his voice much more forceful. "Tell me and I shall allow you to leave unharmed."

Roy allowed himself a semblance of a triumphant smile.

"You can't read my mind," he said. "You aren't all powerful. I'm not telling you anything."

"I am a servant of the Black Hand. Do not tempt me, for I have access to his power."

The creature half turned his back on Roy with a sly look.

"You are Ray McMickle. A serial killer who killed women. You are dead," said Roy, trying to rationalize what it was before him by putting it into words.

"I am much more now, human," he said, with a little derision in his voice. "I must know who brought you here."

"I won't tell you," said Roy, firmly. "How come I'm not dead yet?"

The creature turned his head towards Roy and smiled.

"You kill only women don't you," he said, remembering some visions. "You covet them. You think they're pretty. It feeds your power."

"Men are apes," he said. "Unrueful, dirty creatures."

"So you won't kill me," Roy cut in, "because I am a man."

"Blood is blood," said the creature, "and I will sup on any blood if I feel the urge." He extended a bony, white finger with a sharp little nail at the end of it and pointed at the candle he'd left near his throne. His finger beckoned in a subtle gesture and slowly Roy realized that the light was flowing from the candle to where the vampire stood as though he'd picked up the candle and brought it there himself. And what it illuminated...

"Oh shit..." said Roy.

"It ain't so bad, mon," said Scooter. He was hanging by his arms, his rib cage opened up like the Arc of the Covenant at prayer time. "Dey open you up, and pull out your heart and show it to you while it's still beating, then dey take a bite out of it like it a red, juicy Macintosh."

"Oh, Scooter, man, what did they do to you?" said Roy, his voice hinted with sadness and pleading.

"I told you to get out of here, Roy boy. Dis hot hellhole ain't gonna let you go now, boy. You're trapped here. But it ain't so bad, when dey let you become a vampire. Dey keep you alive for awhile, and make you thirsty for blood. And then dey let you out at night."

"They...?"

"Ya, mon. Dere must be at least-"

He'd taken away the light. The Master of Darkness had doused it and Roy ran forward and cried, "Scooter!" but all he grasped was empty air in front of a dead, grey brick wall.

"You bastard," said Roy under his breath, letting out a quiet sigh. Then, "Another ghost...they're all dead..."

But he looked up and spied that he was near to the stairs. His first urge was to bolt for them but that seemed too easy. How could someone so easily run away from a demon in his own den? And why would he want to? He wasn't really scared anymore, and this was a once in a lifetime chance. Even if it would cost him his life. So he took his eyes off the steps lest he muster any suspicion from the dead serial killer.

He trained his eyes upon Ray McMickle in a bold, hard stare.

"Why me," said Roy. "You brought me here. Why me."

The vampire smiled revealing a row of ghastly white teeth outlined in brown rot. He lifted his hair and it looked as though it moved, as though it were a mass of filthy, demonic snakes.

"I see the well of seething, steaming souls and every once in a while dip my black hand in there and pull one out just for fun. Life is pain, murder is joy. I am much more than a vampire, for I feed off souls as well as blood. And you are a lost soul, lost in Lebanon Junction, Kentucky and in my web."

He had a portentous smile on his face, and he looked directly at Roy for the first time.

"I will show you what pain is..." he said, his voice deep and echoing off the walls of the basement as everything went black around him. All he could do was grasp around for the stairs in the barest hope he could find them.

Fourteen: Family Secrets

The very house itself must have been alive was what Roy thought. For it felt as though it had spit him out from the very mouth of its door, and the windows were eyes that bore down upon him in malice for the crimes he'd committed in the rooms above. Had the vampire possessed that much power as to usher him up the steps and throw him out the door without lifting a finger? To blur his vision and make the great grey whorehouse sway as though it was liquid?

Roy clenched his eyes to clear his head. Then picked his head up and looked around. He was stuck in the proverbial dead of night, and the crickets chirped as though they were violins at the crescendo of a scary moment in a horror film. Why hadn't the vampire killed him? Why had he been thrust back in the creepy cold night under the

167

Kentucky sky? It didn't make sense to him. All his hauntings had pointed to him dying at the hands of the creature that had obviously brought him such erotic and disturbing dreams of ghosts and stories of serial killers. Now he was stuck out here in the night and Roy knew that he could be assaulted psychologically by the effects and nuances of the darkness. But he felt much safer now, because he was out of the reach of that creature. Ray McMickle. Serial killer and rapist, first class misogynist.

Should I run? he wondered. His mood was noncommittal, neither scared nor brave nor confident as he stood there all alone in the night. He might as well have been naked and freshly born. Then the door to the house swung open and smacked shut and a familiar mass of long, wavy red hair cut a dark and trenchant outline in the night.

"Howdy," said Mesmerelda, her voice sombre. Roy didn't answer her, just looked over at her blankly as she moseyed over to him, moving her hips in an all too feminine way. "You going to say anything or just stand there like a mute farm hand."

"You've got a hell of a rodent problem in your basement."

"Amazing you kept your sense of humour," she said, standing in front of him now. "Even though it's deader than any vampire ah've ever met."

"Well, you're old enough to have met one," said Roy.

"Yeah, ah am, aren't I?" said Mesmerelda, nodding her head with him. Then she reared her hand back and stabbed him in the gut with a knife and Roy doubled over in pain, clutching his stomach, but refusing to fall to the ground. "Don't think ah'm doing this just because I am a bitch or something. If you're already in pain then maybe you won't feel it or nothing as much. Don't believe everything you hear in those trashy vampire novels. It ain't all gothic and pretty and sensual. It just hurts. And they ain't all like Ray."

"Oh fuck, oh shit," said Roy, spitting blood on the ground along with his words. "Not you...not you..."

"Yeah, me. Mesmerelda McMickle. This is my house you were in. Ray was my brother, and ah didn't completely lie to you. Ah was friends with Milly Gifford. And you were certainly right. This town is a dead town. And you're about to find out just how right you were..."

Fifteen: The Kentucky Vampire Clan

He'd staggered over to the main street, mainly because he had nowhere else to go. What else was he to do? Let himself be bitten by people all morphed into bats, then offer himself as a pittance to the demigod Ray McMickle? He probably would because he would have no choice and he just couldn't leave. He was a survivor, like Reg and Donny-boy, but only barely. Maybe they were just dumb enough to survive because they were dumb enough to be scared. And Roy had enough brains in his head to step headlong into it all because he refused to believe in fear until he was leaving a bloody trail for a group of hungry vampires to follow.

He staggered his way down the main street and his only blessing of hope would be the red flashing lights of an ambulance. But he got the next best thing: the ghost of Milly Gifford. Though it may not save his life to have her here.

"Oh darlin', what did they do to you," she said, her voice filled with pity. Roy kept staggering forward, thinking he would pass right through her because she was a ghost, but he bumped into what seemed to be solid flesh. "Please don't die on me, Roy, you're so close now. Ah need you badly just for a few more nights."

"C-can't," said Roy, feeling his life leave him with every drip of blood between his fingers. Milly picked his head up with her fingers and brought him close to her lips and kissed him. Her lips were so red it looked as though they'd been painted with blood. "Y-you brought me down th-there," he said. "L-lead me into his c-clutches..."

"No, darlin' that ain't it at all. You have to believe me. See, ah was Ray McMickle's first real sacrifice, and he didn't die when the Sheriff shot him in the back with a shotgun. He rose again and he stole my bones before anyone could bury them proper. That's where he's getting his power from. He put some black magic on me and now he's got to kill and kill just to keep alive. But his power comes from my bones. That's why ah brought you down there, Roy."

"I f-felt everything," he said. "C-can't go b-back there. He'll k-kill me."

"Roy, darlin', you're dead if you stay out here. He's distracted now so I only got a moment where I can talk freely, but ah can't protect you. He'll send his Clan after you."

"C-clan?"

"Yeah. You were right about this town being dead. 'Cause Ray killed them all. After he'd risen from the dead and all, he came back for revenge on the whole lot a them. Clean wiped them out with his own fangs and turned them all to vampires. This is a dead town, Roy. All the people living in it are dead, ghosts, and soon they'll be after you. And there ain't a thing ah can do to help you. You've got to dig up my bones, Roy."

She let him go and he still clutched at his bloody stomach. It spasmed with pain and he felt cold and tingly and his head throbbed from the inside of his temple. He looked up and Milly's ghost was gone. He'd lost a lot of blood. Could all this be another illusion?

Fuck no, he thought. *This goddamn pain in my gut is real.* But everything around him was surreal. The town all devoid of everything but a few people, the fact that he was seemingly trapped within it. Walking down the darkened, dusty street while his guts dripped a path behind him that any vampire worth it's fang would be able to follow. He staggered further along the road and with each step it looked as though he'd keel over and crack his skull on the ground. But that would be too merciful a fate for him. His fate was waiting for him in the streets, watching him stagger to the middle of the road.

"Oh fuck, what is that?" cried Roy, as though his mother would be there to save him from his nightmare. He'd spotted the first of Ray McMickle's Kentucky Vampire Clan, and it wasn't anything so pretty nor nearly as ghoulishly suave as the serial killer himself. The creature stared at him from the recesses of an alcove, half hidden in shadow. It was a sluggish and laggard looking Nosferatu, and it lifted it's long, clawed fingers and licked its slathering lips with big, dirty white fangs protruding out from its mouth.

"Fuck no," said Roy, and he increased the speed of his staggered hop until he reached a jog. Such a futile attempt at escape! For he could barely run faster than a three-legged dog much less an unearthly vampire. "Won't fucking get me dammit."

The vampire left the alcove and moved after him, lifting it's arms to reveal saggy, leathery flesh, filthy and brown like bat's wings. It took to the air and wailed overhead at Roy as he desperately tried to run from the hellish agent of death. He felt the bat wings beat as the presence of the creature loomed just behind him, and he so desperately wished he'd stayed with Reg and Donny-boy instead of chasing his mad obsessions and vaporous dreams.

"I'll never dream again," he cried to himself as he tried to run away from the vampire. As soon as the words left his mouth a guttural, choking screech pierced his ears like someone was being stuck with an eight-inch knitting needle. Even after the screech stopped his ears were consumed by a reverberating ringing which almost drowned out the pain in his stomach. The wind pushed behind him as the vampire made passes at him from the air. But the screech had been a call to arms of sorts, for others began to come out from the shadows; store fronts, houses, the local school...these were the people of Lebanon Junction, Kentucky, and Roy was now their only prey and feast for the night. He had no hope whatsoever and he realized that the knife he'd been stabbed in the gut with might have had some small mercy in it. At least he was already dying.

The first of the Clan swooped in from behind him and shoved him down to the ground. He landed on his shoulder and dislocated it with a crack. He immediately rolled over to his back though his instinctive fear for his life was far outweighed by his morbid curiosity at seeing his killers attack. They swooped in on him like bats, or rather vultures, feeding on his rotting remains. The men lapped up the blood from his wounded stomach and bit his neck, the children bit at his toes and fingers and the women champed gleefully on his cock and nipples. Roy screamed as he felt his body being bitten, tearing the otherwise silent night apart, not even screaming at them to stop, just screaming, "Nooooooo!!!"

What scared him the most was that they didn't bite him deep enough nor hard enough to kill him, and they left him lying there, a ragged, blood-soaked piece of flesh, and he thought he heard Ray McMickle laugh quietly from the dark night sky...

His fingers touched it and it was like sponge cake, but just a little overdone. The edges were rough and crispy and when he pushed on it, it sprang back up like a feathered pillow does. But there were spots like that all over him as though he'd broken out in hives. And the heat beating down upon him made the pain all that much the worse. It had dried the blood and with every movement he made his scabs would tear from his flesh with a squishy, suction-like sound.

He got up and held his head, looked at the wounds all over his body. Nearly every inch of it. Had they left him for dead? Had the sun chased them away before they could finish the job?

He tried to walk. Still he limped and felt the urge to grab his stomach as though a knife was jammed in it. He couldn't help but loll his tongue out as though it too had been bitten. And his face was smeared with dirt, his hair sticking out all mussed up and even torn out in some places.

He staggered down the street and saw a faint flicker of hope in the distance. A saviour of sorts: Smelly Jesus.

Who cares if he stank? Aesthetics was of his least concern now, especially considering the state of his own image.

He was leaning up against a wall of a storefront, quietly playing a soothing and solemn tune on his harmonica. Roy staggered up to him and stood over him, teetering as though he were about to fall. Smelly Jesus stopped playing and looked up at him, squinting his eyes to the sun.

"You come back to be my ridin' partner, mister? 'Cause it's too late, now. You're trapped here. We both are."

Roy tried to speak, stuttering over his swollen tongue.

"Th-there...are...s-sick..."

"You been fightin', mister? Was that all that noise last night?"

"Y-yes..th-there's...got to...get out of...here..."

"That ain't happening," mister. "I told you I can see things, and that ain't one of 'em. I been watching you, mister. You been sleeping aaaalll day. That ain't good. Ain't good at all."

Roy looked up at the sun. Despite the heat he saw that the sun wasn't very high in the sky, that the day was coming to an end once again. He knew that he couldn't endure another night with the Kentucky Vampire Clan after his already shredded carcass.

He walked away from Smelly Jesus and was a little disappointed that he wasn't serenaded with a harmonica haiku. There was something about the stinky bastard that was different. He seemed a bit sombre, reflective.

Roy felt his heart beat. He was at the frayed ends of sanity. He was starving, in pain, and he had no control over the slowly dipping sun that, once gone, meant his certain death.

But what could he do? He was certainly in no condition to dig up Milly's bones, and he had this sinking feeling that they weren't being kept in the cemetery. He felt that Milly had let him experience her rape because her bones had been buried beneath the basement floor to consecrate the demonic hex Ray McMickle had put on the town.

It was much too far to go to Reg and Donny-boy's shack, and he wasn't entirely sure of the direction. He could only stagger up and down Main St., hopeless and lost and trapped, in hopes of finding some food so he could at least have a little comfort before his life was snuffed out by the Clan. He wrapped his arms around his belly and walked.

Violet! came the thought, snapping into his head like a match

bursting when lit. There was someone else he could find! But it meant

going back to the whorehouse anyway, but at least he could avoid the

basement and the serial killer turned blood-sucking vampire Ray

McMickle and walking all over Milly's bones. He walked up Main St.

fast as he could and went over to the grey whorehouse, trying to

disregard that stubborn, gruesome feeling in his gut that he got when its

windows glared down at him. He hid himself behind some bushes just

off the front lawn, trying to stay out of sight in case Mesmerelda

McMickle happened to feel the urge to satisfy her thirst and sip

whiskey on the porch. For who knew what she would do to him if he

were found? And he knew that it was somehow her that had lured him

here in the first place, making herself look young and fuckable as she

strode off the bus shaking her sass at him.

He clenched his bitten hand, thinking to himself in a little bit of

a sick joke how much he'd wished it had only been bees that had

swarmed him, for he had an allergy and would have died much more

painlessly and quickly then he was now. He prayed to himself for a little luck, hoping that this was the time she came in to turn down the bed sheets.

It was dark for a while because he kept passing out, and after a while he didn't even realize it and didn't care. He couldn't stay awake. He kept bumping his head against the tree he was leaning on and rustling the bushes in front of him so as to ruin his efforts at being discreet.

Then he heard the screen door slam just as his head hit the tree again and he tensed himself, hoping it wasn't Mesmerelda. He peeked over the bush and caught a glimpse of Violet's dark hair. He realized that he hadn't actually got a good look at her and didn't really know what she looked like besides her outline.

He waited for her to walk by the bush and when she passed close enough he leaned out and grabbed her ankle, as he didn't have the strength with which to lift himself up off the ground. Violet leapt and let out a little yelp, and Roy waved his hands so as to try and calm her.

"Q-quiet, p-please," he said, barely able to speak because of his swollen, bee-bitten tongue.

"My God, Mr. Stanich, what happened to you?" said Violet, putting a hand daintily to her chest. She was wearing a light lavender top, loosely buttoned, white jean shorts, and sandals that had straps wrapping up over her ankles.

"V-vam-" began Roy, but was unable to continue because he was coughing.

"Mr. Stanich, ah better get you inside and cleaned up and a nice big meal inside of you. C'mon, now, can you walk?"

Roy reached up for her and she helped him up and put his arm around her shoulder for support. She turned him around and he reared back and stopped her.

"N-not th-there, no," he stuttered, gesturing to the whorehouse.

"Ah got to get you inside," said Violet, but Roy was adamant and wouldn't budge despite his weakened and pliant state. "Fine, then, ah guess ah can take you to my house."

She started off down the road and turned him back down Main St. again. There were echoes of the night as twilight began to descend on Lebanon Junction, Kentucky, the stars just barely visible against the turquoise sky that was darkening to azure.

Roy caught himself again as he thought he saw someone looking at him. He only caught a glimpse of the man's scraggly, unkempt dark hair as he disappeared around a corner.

Ghosts, thought Roy. *Town's full of ghosts and killers.*

Violet turned him off of the main road and then brought him to her house and laid him down on the couch. Roy was finally relieved because he could relax and close his eyes without the fear of anything attacking him, and with Violet there he felt he could close his eyes without the fear of letting his life slip away.

"We got to get you washed up," she said, scrounging around in the cupboards. "Ah got some food heating up and ah'll be there in just a sec so you hang tight."

A moment later she came out of the kitchen with a glass of brandy, a wash cloth and a bottle of iodine.

"Ah'll get you some cookies or something to munch on to keep your strength up," she said as she poured iodine all over the wash cloth and bathed his wounds. Roy cringed and made a grunting sound each time Violet put the iodine to his skin but after a while he numbed to the pain and it got easier. Then it was as though she were merely using water to clean him off. "You're looking better already."

"Maybe you should be using holy water," Roy quipped. The juice had stung his tongue but it felt better now and he could kind of talk.

"Wouldn't do a damn a good," said Violet as she cleaned him off. "You feeling any stronger? The cookies helping?" Roy nodded a yes.

"I can't believe what I've seen, Violet," he said, as though he were giving her a dying man's confession. "I don't know how to say this to you, but..."

"Just tell me, Mr. Stanich."

"Vampires. I've seen vampires. They want to kill me slowly and drain my blood."

"Ah know," said Violet, diligently cleaning between his fingers.

"You know about all that?" said Roy, flabbergasted.

"Of course ah do, Mr. Stanich. You don't live in a dead town all your life and not realize a few things. Lean forward a bit." She began to clean behind his ears as well as his neck and shoulders.

"How can you know all this and still live here?" he said, his tone demanding. She stopped wiping his bitten skin for a moment and looked him in the eye.

"You don't realize what all this means, Mr. Stanich. Ah was born into this Hell, but you, now that's a different story. Some of us are survivors here, but ah think that's just about it for Lebanon Junction. Hanging on by a thread. Last ah heard of Reg and Donny-boy they barely get a decent nights sleep and Karl just sits in his gun shop reading the newspaper and shooting anything near threatening him. But you, Mr. Stanich, you wandered in here and got trapped in the spider's web. Ain't good when that happens. Should have just kept moving on. Should have had a path to follow."

Her eyes were a little bit sad as she looked at him, then she pulled her gaze away and leaned over him again in her skimpy southern attire and began cleaning the wounds at his shoulders and back. Roy just let himself be handled as though he were a corpse, staring dead and dumbfounded into the corner of the room. He started to feel the iodine burning into his back like a scorpion's sting, but he ignored it as he tried to figure out this mixed up town.

Violet pulled him further forward so she could reach lower down his back, and Roy felt her hot breath near to his ear now. He couldn't make out any words but he felt something coming from her mouth, falling on his ear like a feather, something wet and sensual and exciting-

"What the hell are you doing?" he said, pushing her away from him. She gave him a blank look of misunderstanding. "I'm sorry. I guess I'm just a bit freaked out. I don't know why, but I don't feel as safe here as I thought I would."

"You aren't safe here. They're going to come get you anyways. You're trapped in Lebanon Junction and if you think the vampires are all dumb creatures you've got to think again. You're lucky you ain't dead already. You still got your soul, Mr. Stanich. And that's something they take very seriously. Now ah'm almost done with your back and the only part left is your...thing and your butt. So just relax or something, have another cookie."

"I don't know how I'm gonna clean that off," said Roy, with a little bit of a mischievous smile. "That's gonna sting like hell."

Violet held out the washcloth and said, "You can try it and if you can't handle it ah'll give you a hand. Don't have to be embarrassed to ask."

Roy tried it. It hurt like hell. He didn't even have to ask Violet. She took the cloth and wiped at his swollen, red penis while he clenched the armrests of the chair in indescribable agony as the pain radiated to every nerve in his body.

"Poor baby," said Violet, but she continued to wipe away at the wounds. Roy clenched his teeth and suppressed a grunt of dire suffering. "Violet'll make it aaaaall better for you."

She finished and then stood up and leaned over him again to wipe off the rest of his back.

"You okay? You want to take a rest for a minute?"

"No," breathed Roy. "I'm, okay."

"Good," she said. "Good boy. The wounds are almost gone. Vampire wounds seem to heal pretty quickly if they don't kill you."

She reached her hand all the way down to the small of his back, trying to cover every inch of his skin though she couldn't see what she was doing too well. Her mouth was at his neck again and he felt her wet breath once more and thought for one moment that her lips grazed the soft flesh there, but he didn't push her away this time. This time he let himself succumb and he hated himself for being that way because it felt like he was succumbing to a vampire. And he didn't want to push her away again because he had no friends here and she was so helpful and he didn't want to seem neurotic or nuts.

"Mr. Stanich," she said, whispering in his ear. "Ah know you're in pain and all, but ah was just wondering if...you know, you might see fit to repay me the favour. Ah'll be real gentle and ah'll stop if you need me to, but seeing as we don't get many men out these parts..."

She stopped talking and kissed his neck and he shuddered. It was almost to the point that his body couldn't distinguish between pleasure and pain anymore.

"Why is it so erotic?" he said, and she held his gaze with a soft, fleeting one of her own.

"The vampires, you mean? Ah guess when you get two bodies so close like that it don't matter if you're killing or you're kissing."

She ushered him off the chair and laid him down on the floor, pulling off his shorts.

"You remember, you tell me if it hurts at all," she said, then smiled. "It's been so long ah don't even have to get myself ready."

She took hold of him gently with her hand, riding the shaft, feeling every bump and bruise and scab, and she bent down and kissed it until he was hard enough for her. She was on her knees as she leaned over him, and then she straightened up and began to undo her lavender top from which her breasts were already bursting.

"Do you like them, Mr. Stanich?" she asked, and he nodded yes timidly. "That's good. Ah know they're nice but sometimes you just got to hear it from someone else. Are you scared or something?"

"Yeah. A little."

"You shouldn't be. Hopefully, in a few minutes, you won't be."

She undid her white shorts and pulled them off, her patch of hair hidden slightly by the shadows her hips made because she was bending a little.

"What about this?" she said. "Do you like this too?" Again Roy nodded nervously. "You just relax now, Mr. Stanich, just let me take care of you."

She straddled him, and he looked at her thighs lusciously, as they were ready to wrap around his hips, at her full breasts as they hung from her chest, the nipples staring at him. Violet paused a moment, looking at his face, wondering why everything about his expression said he was uncertain as to whether he wanted to do this. How could any man possibly resist her lust proffered? Especially with her succulent body about to be draped all over him.

She took hold of him once more, gently between her thumb and forefinger, and angled his sex until it lined up with hers. Then she slipped him into her pocket and slowly slid down on him, being careful not to damage him further. Violet sighed and let out a quiet little groan, and wrapped her arms around herself, squeezing her breasts until they spilled out. Slowly up and down on him she went, enjoying the sensation of being with a man and she so wanted to hug him but for some reason she didn't, she simply enjoyed the sex. And she looked down at him and his face oscillated between expressions of pain and sadness and pleasure.

"Mr. Stanich," she said. "Do you mind if ah hold you? For real, like." He nodded acceptance and she bent down, her breasts dangling

189

for a moment until they were crushed between the two of them. They

felt so warm and comforting against his chest, and her arms around

him were like the arms of a mother carefully guarding her child.

"Thank you, Mr. Stanich," she said, whispering, her lips near to

his ear as she started moving again, slowly. "This means a lot to me."

And after a few moments he put his arms around her, but he

didn't really know why. Perhaps it was because he was in such pain that

he found relief in succumbing to the ultimate, fleshly pleasure. Or

perhaps it was because she was human, and so absolutely real. His

fingers traced lines up and down her back with each meticulous motion

of her hips, feeling every groove of her soft, tanned skin. It felt nice to

have a human being to hold onto, and it made him feel safe despite the

fact that the Kentucky Vampire Clan could be breathlessly salivating,

slathering tongues dripping and rubbing their hands with glee right

outside the door.

"Mr. Stanich?" said Violet. "Do you mind if ah ask what it feels

like for you? If that's not getting too intimate for you."

"Why do you want to know?"

"Ah just do. Ah guess on account of me seducing you and all. If you like what it is ah'm doing."

"It feels...I don't know...perfect, I guess. Like I'm in another world and I don't have any problems. Like I'm not lost anymore."

"That's good. Ah like to hear that. Do you think you have enough strength to finish?"

"Yeah," said Roy, and took hold of her shoulders as she began to move a little faster. She got close to him again and whispered his name in his ear, then kissed it and slathered all over it with her tongue. Her hips put a very firm pressure on his and he knew that his climax might be a little bit painful. He felt his heart thumping and every wound on his body throbbing and crying out for blood like a thousand hungry mouths and Violet was kissing his neck and it hurt and she kissed, sharp, hurtful pain and suffering and he tried to push her away but she was clamped at his hips and teeth champed his neck and-

"What the fuck are you doing?" he cried. He held her at arms length away, pushing her up by her shoulders. He was still inside her though, and he didn't have the strength to throw her off. He felt himself about to lose control and was filled with self-loathing at the fact

that he wouldn't be able to stop his gift from being given.

"Please, Mr. Stanich, ah just want a taste," she said.

"Oh, fuck, you're one of them! Get off of me!"

"Ah'm not letting you go until you finish." Because then she

would have him, mind, body and soul. Roy gritted his teeth trying to

resist the urge, impossibly, and he felt some seeping out of him as

Violet began to thrash her hips around violently.

"No, fuck you, hell no," he said, starting to cry. He tried to look

at her face through his tears though every notion of his heart wanted to

look away. He caught skewed and watery glimpses of her and saw the

salacious, iniquitous expression on her face, her tongue hanging out,

her eyes wide. But her teeth, they weren't fangs. She was still human.

But Roy hadn't the strength to push her away. Nor the strength to resist

ejaculation (as if any man ever did.) As he climaxed within her she

found a way to circumvent the strength of his arms. She all but fell

upon him and took a healthy champ at his neck, and Roy finally found

the will to separate their bodies and the momentum to roll her off of

him. "You bitch, you're one of them."

192

"No ah'm not, but ah'm learning, slowly. You're right the town's dead, Mr. Stanich, but there are a few survivors. And you've met them all. Karl mostly shoots anything that gets near him, but soon he's going to run out of bullets. Reg and Donny-boy...well, they don't have much will power. That's why they're keeping me human for a while and teaching me. Soon old Reg'll get a taste of what you just had, and then nothing'll be left of old Lebanon Junction, Kentucky. Place is just hanging by a thread as it is, just waiting for the Kentucky Vampire Clan to take over."

"You're a sick witch if you'll fuck that oversized greasy hick pig," said Roy, rubbing at the wound at his neck. It was superficial, like he'd cut himself shaving.

"Hey, a cock is a cock and blood is blood," she said, gesturing in a laissez-faire manner as she stood there stark naked. "As long as ah get mine." She reached over to a side table and picked up a knife hidden within a vase. "Now, are you going to give me a taste or are we going to have to do this the hard way?"

Sixteen: The Master Plan & The Sinister Clan

Lebanon Junction, Kentucky was a bit of an aberration. For one thing, there were only a few people left in the town, for it had been cursed many years ago by Ray McMickle's killing spree, his murderous Satanic rage. The few stragglers who hadn't yet bit the bullet and passed over to mindless vampirism were just stubborn folk. Karl, who sat reading old newspapers over and over and pointlessly shooting the vampires of the Clan who tried to feast upon his body and make him one of them; Reg and Donny-boy, who were too stupid to live but just smart enough not to die; and Violet, the girl who was about Milly's age when she died and was being eagerly tutored by Ray McMickle himself to become a vampire. If only Violet could see ghosts the way Stanich did. If only she could speak to them.

But she belonged to a serial killer turned vampire now, a guy who liked to touch her tits when he tutored her, who liked to pinch at her pussy and call it magic. Made her feel better when he took little licks of her blood, merely because he said it would. And she believed him. In one sense she was fortunate. She reminded Ray of Milly and for that reason she would have a little magic of her own and wouldn't merely become bitten and turned into a mindless creature hungry for blood. She would be dead, but she would retain her brain, though it would shrivel after being drenched in the evil of the Black Hand.

Sometimes people get lost in this world, and they disappear off the face of it. The decision may be a voluntary and conscious one, and it is the persons themselves who makes the decision to leave society and wander the wretched fringes of it, like Roy Stanich. Some view society from a high perch, and when they lean over the edge to see how far the fall is, someone puts a boot to their ass and gives them a push over the edge, like Smelly Jesus. People who leave society are an aberration themselves and usually end up dead. Doctors call it suicide and write it off as a medical anomaly of nature. God calls it purgatory.

Steve Zinger

When an aberration meets an aberration the resulting mixture usually results with some sort of chaos. The explosion was on the surface of Roy Stanich's brain, and he truly felt the repercussions within his soul. He became one of the town of Lebanon Junction, Kentucky. It owned him. He finally realized that now, as he crawled along Main St., the air dusty as it infested his new wounds with filth. Violet had stabbed him thirty times with a one-inch blade and when he fell to the ground she licked his body up and down like a Popsicle. But she didn't kill him, for his body belonged to Ray McMickle, his mind to the Black Hand. She dragged him out on the road and gave him a swift kick in the ass so he went face first into the dirt and had to spit out the filth. She left him there for the Clan. Roy looked back, seeing Violet rushing back inside her house. It was her heart's desire to be part of the Kentucky Vampire Clan but even she feared it immeasurably.

Roy picked up his head as he crawled along the dirty street, feeling filth between his fingers, and saw with much more clarity the aberration of the town of Lebanon Junction. It was as though a small piece of desert had infected the lush, green growth of Kentucky. All around were rolling hills carpeted with thick bush and dense forests,

196

but the roads of Lebanon Junction were looking mighty dusty and barren. Had Ray McMickle's curse infected the very land itself? Did he suck the waters from the roots of the trees too? Did Lebanon Junction exist just beyond the realm of human perception, impossible to find unless one's soul was lost or the Kentucky Vampire Clan smelled blood and sucked you in forever?

One of the creatures had come out to watch him, perhaps because it still retained some intelligence from it's humanity, and therefore was curious. Roy continued to crawl. Such a futile, laborious effort! But it was all he could do, being so near to being broken. The vampire side-stepped it's way up to him, it's skin cold, blue and desiccated and oversized hands hanging from its side with thick, cumbersome claws made especially for slashing.

"Yes, Mr. McMickle, you have reached me and I am Satan, or the Black Hand as some may call me. You have succeeded in cursing an entire town, infecting it with the vampire virus so that they are dead but not quite dead and need human blood. Now what I can do for you is get you all set up with a TX437 model vampire, just perfect for the man who wants a mindless army of the night. Is that a twinkle I see in your eye Mr. McMickle? Well don't shine yet! Wait until I fill you in

on the details: this vampire comes with a sharp set of teeth all the way

around the upper and lower palette, excellent for any morsel of flesh

that somehow may be regurgitated. Immediately upon the point of

turning, the skin turns a sickly blue and the hair falls out. And the ears,

the ears get just a little bit pointy, like the classic Nosferatu! And you

don't even have to worry about any copyright infringement or anything

like that. Every lawyer on the face of the earth has already sold their

soul to me!

"Now the best part about it is what happens to the brain. It

shrivels back to the size of a monkey! No petty squabbles or

insubordination in the ranks. All you have to do is keep them supplied

with steady morsels of flesh and engorged with blood. Be sure to gorge

them at least once a year, that's guaranteed to keep them happy. And I

know, Mr. McMickle, my delicious, capricious serial killer, that you are

wondering how much all this costs. Why, merely the price of sending

me the lost souls! That's it! It couldn't be simpler! It's something you

already have a knack for! Of course I would have to hold your soul as collateral but when you get a bargain like this that is merely a formality...

One tends to imagine things when one is in pain. The vampire was gnawing at his arm the way a beaver gnaws bark on wood-without care and no disdain for the log in it's hands. He laughed at his own thoughts and saw his own hand out of the corner of his eye and it was black. Like someone had burnt it in a fire or carved it from the cooled coals. And the rest of it was being gnawed upon, and Roy could only laugh and wait for the rest of the townspeople to come out and form a Clan and feast upon his body. He laughed because he was still alive.

Then he heard a clap. And the pain stopped, but he hardly noticed that because he was so numb it felt as though he were laying on pins and needles and his arm throbbed dully as though anesthetized. He looked at his hand again. It looked normal. He whispered for Milly even though he knew she couldn't help him for she was a ghost and could only show him the most burning image of her life-her last days as an unwilling slut of Satan and her love and her murder.

"Pick up your head."

Steve Zinger

The voice was surreal and deep as though the sound came through a megaphone. Roy hadn't the strength to obey and a hand took hold of his sweaty hair and pulled his head up. "You have come to me to beg, Stanich."

"Al...ready...dead...won't beg...for my...life..."

"I never said I would make you beg for your life. I would just make you beg. Matters not to me if you are dead or alive, your soul throbs inside and burns and it is mine. Psychological instability you think but it is magic and Satan and my devil-may-care glee as I grind my boot to the nerves of your damnation! I will see you scream my name and be my salvation for another year because you are mine."

Roy opened his mouth slowly, his throat feeling as though someone had pierced the back of it with a toothpick, and made as though to speak. Ray McMickle, the vicious and victorious serial killer long shot dead and saved from the bullet by Satan did him the honour of being his audience for what may be his final words.

And Roy stuck his tongue out at him.

McMickle dropped Roy's head into the dirt on the road, nearly disgusted at the man's resolve. He walked away in angry dejection and

200

consternation, his black robes trailing him and his skin glowering a
sickly, pale white.

"You know not what you see! I see the Black Hand! I have it's
power! A big splash will be mine! Blood on blood on blood and down
my throat and only a pittance for the poor people of the town. But you,
you cannot see. Every ceremony starts with a ritual. The Black Hand
needs his offering. I must give to remain what I am, lest my bones be
crushed to powder in his fingers." Ray McMickle extended a bony,
clawed hand and lifted Roy's head up from a distance. Roy saw him
there and felt what he did. His neck was cold. "You know not what you
see," he reiterated. It felt to Roy that his head would at any moment
become separated from his body.

"I...love her..." he said. McMickle spun and his yellow eyes
grew bright with anger, the black slits turning to fiery crimson.

"No!" he cried. "You are a lost soul! You have fallen from
God's grace! You know not what you see!"

"I can see...ghosts," he said, struggling to get the words out as
his life flickered like a candle next to an open window at the blackest
point of night. "And I...love her."

"NO! You are desolate! You are dying! Forsake your unrequited love in the vain hope of maintaining a finger hold in this world!" cried McMickle as he pointed his claws dramatically and demonically at Roy. "You have no plan! You are lost! Dying!"

"No...I will...never...give my soul to you," said Roy, feeling his neck being pulled back even further. "This is all...illusion...I don't believe..any of it..."

McMickle went over to him and knelt among his robes at the head of his fallen quarry and looked into his black and desolate eyes and grinned a felonious grin. He saw defeat in this animal's eyes, for the man was battered and broken and his body littered with lacerations. He saw not the faintest spark of hope for it was the last hope, which was kept within the human heart; the human heart from which he would take a voracious and luscious bite.

"There...is nothing for you here...I...am just going to...crawl...up and down...the street until I...die...and there will be no life...left for you...to consume..."

"And be that you die I will still consume your soul as it leaves your body and my Clan will tear you limb from limb with their teeth before you have a chance to see that hope which you pathetically call sunlight."

"But I realize...what I saw...now...the ghosts..."

"Not thinking that this is illusion are we?" said the serial killer, and tittered triumphantly. "Feel my hand on your cheek, rotten. So cold! So prickly! So <u>dead</u>!" He lolled out his cold, lump of a tongue, like a swollen serpent grasping for a rat.

"I saw...*your* ghost...too...walking the streets...you are trapped...like Milly...and I *have*...got a plan..."

The vampire/serial killer Ray McMickle's eyebrow raised like a hairy caterpillar on his crinkled, dead, blue/white forehead in blunt curiosity.

"May...not be able...to save Milly's...bones...to release her truly," stammered Roy, "but...I can love... her memory. And I finally...have...a plan."

"You lie, human," said the Kentucky Vampire. "You try to deceive me to save yourself. And deception is the way of the Black Hand."

Roy smirked through his shredded, blood-caked face, the wounds on his lips cracking though his smile was only subtle, and he told the vampire his plan:

"I am going to...write some best-selling novels...have a torrid love affair...with a comedian's wife...and drop dead when I'm fifty...because of my excesses..."

"Noooooooooooooo!" cried McMickle, gripping his claws to his forehead so tight that he opened the wounds that had been made by years of sleeping in the dirt.

"You...are illusion...I will...die here...and keep my soul. I have seen your ghost too. I know the secret. My neck is bleeding," said Roy.

McMickle's scream echoed and faded into the night and his body became mist and followed the scream to the sky. Roy saw pairs of jaundiced eyes blinking at him from recesses of shadows, from around corners and from shop doorways. The Kentucky Vampire Clan was watching him and he could sense their hunger rising like a witch's broth about to boil over. His head dropped to the filthy ground and he wasn't exactly sure if he had just passed out or finally died...

Seventeen: The Annual Woolly Worm Festival

He was roused by the sound of cars going by. It was a very unexpected sound to hear several of them, for in all his time here he heard barely a one.

"You finally awake now, mister?"

He smelt the stench of Smelly Jesus and coughed. He picked his head up and it throbbed in pain. He looked at the sun and saw people in the town but he didn't even try to smile. But he knew now that he was free of his nightmares.

"How you feeling?" asked the derelict.

"Like I just came out of one of Hitler's showers," said Roy.

"You seemed to be having one hell of a night there, mister. Out in the middle of the road and thrashing around. You lucky I was here to come get you. Darn woke me up but good."

"Sorry," said Roy. "I was having a terrible dream. All about-"

"Ghosts? Vampires?" said Smelly Jesus.

"Yeah," said Roy. "How did you..."

"I told you I could see things, mister. That I knew things. You should have been my riding partner. I'd take a look at yourself if I was you."

Roy pulled his sleeves and his shirt and looked at his legs. He was bitten all up and down his body with the familiar and vicious fang marks of the Kentucky Vampire Clan.

"Oh fuck," he said, crying in anger. "It's real. Shit, it's real. I thought it had all been some sick dream..."

Smelly Jesus took a bite of an onion and said, "You should've stuck with me, mister. I told you I know things. That's why I survived the night. Even Superman had a weakness. Any traveling fool knows vampires can't stand the smell of onions. Makes them sick to their stomach. And <u>you</u> just thought I stank."

But Roy wasn't paying attention.

"All these cars," he said, as several more came driving in. He put his hands to his head and tried to remember his nocturnal insanity.

"Besides, a few days from now, these streets are going to be packed with people!" said Milly, in her usual excited way. Roy stopped walking again.

"What do you mean?"

"For the Woolly Worm Festival! People come 'round here miles every year for the festival. If there's one reason Lebanon Junction, Kentucky exists it's for that festival."

"All you have to do is keep them supplied with steady morsels of blood and be sure to gorge them at least once a year, that's guaranteed to keep them happy."

"Oh God, no," breathed Roy. "All these people." He got up and started into a run to warn the tourists of the impending danger they were walking into. He knew they would disbelieve him but he didn't care how silly he looked. He had the physical evidence tattooed all over his body to prove his story.

He got five feet, then fell to the ground. Deputy Kuthrow had been spying on him from around the corner, waiting for him to come to realization of the facts, and when Roy had bolted he tripped him and pistol-whipped him on the back of the head.

Roy tried to lift himself up and rub the back of his swollen, aching neck but a boot was put to his back and he was pushed to the ground again, able only to endure his pain.

"I've got to go warn those people," he said. "They're in grave danger." He made a move again and the Deputy stepped on his fingers until he heard bone splintering against bone and Roy cried out in pain.

"What seems to be the rush, son?" said the Deputy.

"Vampires..." said Roy, gritting his teeth and struggling to get his fingers out from beneath the shiny black boot. "Town's infested with them."

The Deputy laughed.

"You know, son, it's a funny thing. Every year we get about five, six hundred people coming in from all over to this God-forsaken, backwards, no name ghost town called Lebanon Junction. Place ain't even on a map. So they come, they hear about it from word of mouth and all, to watch our Woolly Worm Festival. You know what that is son? They watch three worms inch their way up some string and the first one to the top wins! There is some gambling of course, and some husbands sneak away over to old Mesmerelda's, and then when the fun's over we treat them to a nice, rib-smacking barbecue. Fatten them up real good. Now this takes us to about, oh say...couple hours after sundown. Most people call home and say they're staying the night in some place that hardly no one's even heard of. Can't ever seem to find it on any map, either."

The Deputy took his foot off of Roy's hand, knelt next to his head and pulled out a dull and rusty old pocket-knife.

"And you know what, son? Most of them never see the light of day again, and the real world just darn can't seem to remember nothing about them. No one ever comes looking for them. No one ever know's they're gone. They die, and, unlike you, they just never know the difference. Some would say that might just be a happy little coincidence, or even that it might just be *too* convenient for our quaint little town here. But if you've lived as long as I have you know that most things in this world never happen by accident."

He pulled off his sunglasses and Roy looked into his jaundiced, yellow eyes...

He said, "Welcome to Mile 0..."

Visit: www.stevezinger.com

Steve Zinger

About the Author

Steve Zinger is a Canadian horror writer with a deep-rooted interest in the American South. In researching this book he made three separate trips to Kentucky, and he often visits the places he writes about before, during and after completing a novel.

He lives and works in Toronto.

Printed in the United States
16813LVS00005B/259-405